"Oh, the poor dear, is she bad? And just as she was doing so nicely, too…"

Dr. Thomas Winters looked stern and angry and his eyes were like granite. Isobel thought it very likely that he had come against his will because Nanny had insisted. She said kindly, in her gentle voice, "I'm indeed sorry to hear about Nanny, but I can't come with you. You know I go where the agency sends me and I just came back from a case. I'm sure if you phone them they'll have a nurse free."

He gave her a thin smile. "My dear Isobel, you underestimate me. I have already arranged with the agency that you'll return with me this evening."

Her eyes grew round. "The arrogance of it!" she declared. "I may refuse a case, you know, Dr. Winters, and I'm doing just that."

"You won't do that." His voice was quiet. "You're a kind and gentle girl. I'm sorry if I've made you angry, but Nanny is ill, and I did not bring her all this way to see her slip through my fingers."

Romance readers around the world were sad to note the passing of **Betty Neels** in June 2001. Her career spanned thirty years, and she continued to write into her ninetieth year. To her millions of fans, Betty epitomized the romance writer, and yet she began writing almost by accident. She had retired from nursing, but her inquiring mind still sought stimulation. Her new career was born when she heard a lady in her local library bemoaning the lack of good romance novels. Betty's first book, *Sister Peters in Amsterdam,* was published in 1969, and she eventually completed 134 books. Her novels offer a reassuring warmth that was very much a part of her own personality. She was a wonderful writer, and she will be greatly missed. Her spirit and genuine talent will live on in all her stories.

THE BEST *of*

BETTY NEELS

NEVER SAY GOODBYE

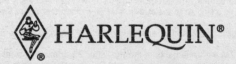

HARLEQUIN®

TORONTO • NEW YORK • LONDON
AMSTERDAM • PARIS • SYDNEY • HAMBURG
STOCKHOLM • ATHENS • TOKYO • MILAN • MADRID
PRAGUE • WARSAW • BUDAPEST • AUCKLAND

ISBN 0-373-47062-2

NEVER SAY GOODBYE

First North American Publication 1999.

Copyright © 1983 by Betty Neels.

This edition published by arrangement with Harlequin Books S.A.

® and TM are trademarks of the publisher. Trademarks indicated with ® are registered in the United States Patent and Trademark Office, the Canadian Trade Marks Office and in other countries.

www.eHarlequin.com

Printed in U.S.A.

CHAPTER ONE

THE HOUSE, one of a row of similar Regency houses in an exclusive area of London, gave no hint from its sober exterior as to the magnificence of its entrance hall, with its imposing ceiling and rich carpet, nor even more to the equally imposing room, the door to which an impassive manservant was holding open. Isobel Barrington walked past him and, obedient to his request that she should take a seat, took one, waiting until he had closed the door soundlessly behind him before getting up again and beginning a slow prowl round the room. It was a very elegant room, with watered silk panelled walls, a marble fireplace and some intimidating armchairs of the French school, covered in tapestry. The rest of the furniture was Chippendale with nothing cosy about it, although she had to admit that it was charming. Not her kind of room, she decided with her usual good sense; it would do very well for people as elegant as itself; the kind who thought of Fortnum and Mason as their local grocer and understood every word of an Italian opera when they went to one.

She began to circle the room, looking at the profusion of portraits on its walls; gentlemen with unyielding faces in wigs and a variety of uniforms, all sharing the same handsome features; ladies, surprisingly enough, with scarcely a pretty face between them, although they were all sweet as to expression. Isobel, studying a young woman in an elaborate Edwardian dress, concluded that the men of the family had good looks enough and could afford to marry plain wives. 'Probably they were heiresses,' she told herself, and sat down again.

She might not match the room for elegance, but she shared a lack of good looks with the various ladies hanging on its walls. She was on the small side, with a neat figure and nice legs and a face which missed prettiness by reason of too wide a mouth and too thin a nose, although her skin was as clear as a child's and her blue eyes held a delightful twinkle upon occasion. She was dressed in a plain blue dress and looked as fresh and neat as anyone could wish. She put her purse on the small table beside her and relaxed against the chair's high back. When the door opened she sat up and then got to her feet with a calm air of assurance.

'Miss Barrington?' The man who spoke could have been any one of the gentlemen hanging on the walls; he had exactly the same good looks and forbidding expression, although his greying hair was cropped short and his clothes, exquisitely tailored, were very much in the modern fashion.

Isobel met his dark, impersonal stare with a steady look. 'Yes,' she said. 'And you are Dr Winter?'

He crossed the room and stopped before her, a very tall, largely built man in his thirties. He didn't answer her but observed coldly: 'The Agency assured me that they were sending a sensible, experienced nurse with a placid disposition.'

She eyed him with a gentle tolerance which made him frown. She said kindly: 'I'm a sensible woman and I have eight years' experience of nursing and I am of a placid disposition, if by that you mean that I don't take exception to rudeness or get uptight if things go a little wrong...' She added: 'May I sit down?'

The frown became thunderous. 'I beg your pardon, Nurse, please do take a chair...' He didn't sit himself, but began to wander about the room. Presently he said: 'You're not at all the kind of nurse I intended to take with me. Have you travelled?'

'No, but I've nursed in a variety of situations, some of them rather out of the ordinary way of things.'

'You're too young.' He stopped marching around the room and looked at her.

'I'm twenty-five—a sensible age, I should have thought.'

'Women at any age are not always sensible,' he observed bitterly.

Isobel studied him carefully. An ill-tempered man, she judged, but probably just and fair-minded with it, in all probability he was a kind husband and father. She said calmly: 'Then it really doesn't matter what age I am, does it?'

He smiled, and his face was transformed so that she could see that he could be quite charming if he wished. 'All the same—' he began and then stopped

as the door opened and the manservant came in, murmured quietly and went away again.

'You must excuse me for a moment, Miss—er—
Barrington. I shan't be more than a few minutes.'

She was left to contemplate the portraits of his an-
cestors on the walls, although she didn't pay much
attention to them; she had too much to think about.
It was a severe blow if he didn't give her the job...she
needed it badly enough. When she had left hospital
to take up agency nursing, she hadn't had her heart
in it: she had loved her work as Male Surgical Ward
Sister and her bedsitting room in the nurses' home
and going home for her weekends off. However,
when her only, younger brother Bobby had been
given the chance of going to a public school and her
mother had confided to her that there wasn't enough
money to send him, she had given up her post, put
her name down at a nursing agency and by dint of
working without breaks between cases had earned
enough to get Bobby started.

She didn't really enjoy it. It was a lonely life and
she had far less free time; on the other hand, she could
earn almost twice as much money and she had no
need to pay for her food and room. And she wouldn't
have to do it for ever. Bobby was a bright boy, he
was almost certain to get a place in one of the uni-
versities in four or five years' time and then she
would go back to hospital life once more. She should
have liked to marry, of course, but she had no illu-
sions about her looks, and although she could sew
and cook and keep house she had never got to know

a man well enough for him to appreciate these qualities. It was a regret that she kept well hidden, and it had helped to have a sense of humour and a placid nature as well as a strong determination to make the best of things.

She braced herself now for Dr Winter's refusal of her services, and when he came back into the room looking like a thundercloud, she gave an inward resigned sigh and turned a calm face to him.

'That was the nursing agency,' he said shortly. 'They wanted to know if I was satisfied with you for the job I had in mind, and when I said I'd expected someone older and more experienced they regretted that there was positively no one else on their books.' He cast her an exasperated look. 'I intend to leave England in two days' time, and there's no opportunity of finding someone else in forty-eight hours...I shall have to take you.'

'You won't regret it,' she assured him briskly. 'Perhaps you would tell me exactly what kind of case I'm to nurse.'

'An old lady crippled with arthritis. My old nurse, in fact.'

The idea of this self-assured giant of a man having a nanny, even being a small boy, struck Isobel as being faintly ludicrous, but the look that he bent upon her precluded even the faintest of smiles. He sat down at last in one of the Chippendale chairs, which creaked under his weight. 'She married a Pole and has lived in Gdansk since then. Her husband died last year and I've been trying since then to get a permit

for her to return to England. I've now succeeded and
intend to bring her back with me. You will understand
that I shall require a nurse to accompany me; she's
unable to do much for herself.'

'And when do we get back to England?' Isobel
asked.

'I shall want your services only until such time as
a suitable companion for her can be found.' He
crossed one long leg over the other and the chair
creaked again. 'We fly to Stockholm where we stay
the night at a friend's flat and take the boat the following day to Gdansk, we shall probably be a couple
of days there and return to Stockholm and from there
fly back to England. A week should suffice.'

'Why are we not to fly straight to Gdansk? And
straight back here again?'

'Mrs Olbinski is a sick woman; it's absolutely necessary that she should travel as easily as possible; we
shall return by boat to Stockholm and spend at least
a day there so that she can rest before we fly back
here. And we spend a day in Stockholm so that the
final arrangements for her can be made.'

He got up and wandered to the window and stood
staring out. 'You have a passport?'

'No, but I can get one at the Post Office.'

He nodded. 'Well, this seems the best arrangement
in the circumstances; not exactly as I would have
wished, but I have no alternative, it seems.'

'You put it very clearly, Dr Winter,' said Isobel.
Her pleasant voice was a little tart. 'Do you want to

make the arrangements for the journey now, or notify the agency?'

'I'll contact the agency tomorrow.' He glanced at the watch on his wrist. 'I have an appointment shortly and can spare no more time. You will get your instructions, Miss—er—Barrington.'

She got to her feet. 'Very well, Dr Winter—and the name is Barrington, there's no *er* in front of it.' She gave him a vague smile and met his cold stare and walked to the door. 'You would like me to wear uniform, I expect?' And when he didn't answer, she said in patient explanation: 'It might help if you had any kind of difficulties with the authorities...'

'You're more astute than I'd thought, Miss Barrington.' He smiled thinly. 'That's exactly what I would wish you to do.'

He reached the door slightly ahead of her and opened it. 'Perhaps you would confine your luggage to one case? I'll fill in details during the flight.'

The manservant was hovering in the splendid hall. 'Oh, good,' said Isobel cheerfully. 'One wants to know something about a case before taking it on. Goodbye, Dr Winter.' She smiled kindly at him and made an exit as neat and unremarkable as herself.

She took a bus, a slow-moving journey of half an hour or more, back to her home—a small terraced house on the better side of Clapham Common. It looked exactly like the houses on either side of it, but in the narrow hall there was a difference. In place of the usual hallstand and telephone table there was a delicate wall table with rather a nice gilded mirror above it, and the small sitting room into which she hurried was furnished with what their neighbours referred to disparagingly as old bits and pieces, but which were, in fact, the remnants of furniture saved from the sale of her old home some ten years earlier. She never went into the little house without nostalgia for the comfortable village house she had been born and brought up in, but she never mentioned this; her mother, she felt sure, felt even worse about it than she did.

Her mother was sitting at the table, sewing, a small woman with brown hair a good deal darker than her daughter's, the same blue eyes and a pretty face. She looked up as Isobel went in and asked: 'Well, darling, did you get the job?'

Isobel took off her shoes and curled up in a chair opposite her mother. 'Yes, but it's only for a week or two, though. Dr Winter isn't too keen on me, but there wasn't anyone else. I'm to go to Poland with him to fetch back his old nanny.'

Her mother looked faintly alarmed. 'Poland? But isn't that...' she paused, 'well, eastern Europe?'

'He's got a permit for her to come to England to live. Her husband died last year and she's crippled with arthritis, that's why I'm to go with him; she'll need help with dressing and so on, I expect.'

'And this Dr Winter?'

'Very large and tall, unfriendly—to me at any rate, but then he expected someone older and impressive, I think. He's got a lovely house. I'm to be told all the details at the agency tomorrow and be ready to travel in two days—in uniform.'

Her mother got up. 'I'll get the tea. Is he elderly?'

Isobel thought. 'Well, no; he's a bit grey at the sides, but he's not bald or anything like that. I suppose he's getting on for forty.'

'Married?' asked her mother carelessly as she went to the door.

'I haven't an idea, but I should think so—I mean, I shouldn't think he would want to live in a great house like that on his own, would you?'

She followed her mother into the little kitchen and put on the kettle, and while it boiled went into the minute garden beyond. It was really no more than a patch of grass and a flower bed or two but it was full of colour and well kept. There was a tabby cat lying between the tulips and forget-me-nots. Isobel said: 'Hullo, Blossom,' and bent to inspect the small rose bushes she cherished when she was home. They were nicely in bud and she raised her voice to say to her mother, 'They'll be almost out by the time I get back. It's June next week.'

She spent her evening making a list of the things she would need to take with her; not many, and she hesitated over packing a light jacket and skirt. Dr Winter had said uniform, but surely if they were to stay in Stockholm for a day, she need not wear uniform, nor for that matter on the flight there. Perhaps the agency would be able to tell her.

The clerk at the agency was annoyingly vague, offering no opinion at all but supposing it didn't matter and handing Isobel a large envelope with the remark that she would probably find all she wanted to know inside it. Isobel annoyed the lady very much by sitting down and reading the contents through, for, as she pointed out in her sensible way, it would be silly to get all the way home and discover that some vital piece of information was missing.

There was nothing missing; her ticket, instructions on how to reach Heathrow and the hour at which she was to arrive and where she was to go when she got there, a reminder that she must bring a Visitor's Passport with her, a generous sum of money to pay for her expenses and a brief note, typed and signed T. Winter, telling her that she had no need to wear uniform until they left Stockholm. Isobel replaced everything in the envelope, wished the impatient lady behind the desk a pleasant day and went off to the Post Office for her passport. She had to have photos for it, of course. She went to the little box in a corner of the Post Office and had three instant photos taken; they were moderately like her, but they hardly did her pleasant features justice—besides, she looked surprised and her eyes were half shut. But since the clerk at the counter didn't take exception to them, she supposed they would do. Her mother, naturally enough, found them terrible; to her Isobel's unassuming face was beautiful.

She left home in plenty of time, carrying a small suitcase and a shoulder bag which held everything she might need for the journey. After deliberation she had worn a coffee-coloured pleated skirt, with its matching loose jacket and a thin cotton top in shrimp pink, and in her case she had packed a second top and a Liberty print blouse, and because she had been told at the agency that the Scandinavian countries could be cool even in May and June, she had packed a thick hooded cardigan she had bought with her Christmas money at Marks and Spencer.

She took the underground to Heathrow and then found her way to departure number two entrance and went to stand, as she had been told to, on the right side of the entrance. She was ten minutes early and she stood, not fidgeting at all, watching the taxis drawing up and their passengers getting out. She hadn't been there above five minutes when she was startled to hear Dr Winter's deep voice behind her.

'Good morning, Miss Barrington. We will see to the luggage first, if you will come with me.'

Her good morning was composed, a porter took her case and she went across to the weigh-in counter for their luggage to be taken care of, handed her ticket to the doctor and waited until the business had been completed, studying him while she did so.

He was undoubtedly a very good-looking man, and the kind of man, she fancied, who expected to get what he wanted with the least possible fuss. He looked in a better temper, she was relieved to see; it made him look a good deal younger and the tweed suit he was wearing, while just as elegantly cut as the formal grey one he had worn at interview, had the effect of making him seem more approachable.

'Well, we'll go upstairs and have coffee while we

wait for our flight.' He spoke pleasantly and Isobel didn't feel the need to answer, only climbed the stairs beside him, waited a few moments while he bought a handful of papers and magazines and went on up another flight of steps to the coffee lounge, where he sat her down, fetched their coffee and then handed her the *Daily Telegraph* and unfolded *The Times* for himself.

Isobel, who had slept badly and had a sketchy breakfast, drank her coffee, thankfully, sat back in her chair, folded the newspaper neatly and closed her eyes. She was almost asleep at once and the doctor, glancing up presently, blinked. He was by no means a conceited man, but he couldn't remember, offhand, any woman ever going to sleep in his company. He overlooked the fact that he had made no attempt to entertain her.

Isobel, while no beauty, looked charming when she slept, her mouth had opened very slightly and her lashes, golden-brown and very long, lay on her cheeks, making her look a good deal younger than her twenty-five years. Dr Winter frowned slightly and coughed. Isobel's eyes flew open and she sat up briskly. 'Time for us to go?' she enquired.

'No—no. I'm sorry if I disturbed you. I was surprised...'

She gave him her kind smile. 'Because I went to sleep. I'm sure girls don't go to sleep when they're with you.' To make herself quite clear, she added: 'Nurses when you're lecturing them, you know. I expect you're married.'

His look was meant to freeze her bones, only she wasn't that kind of a girl. She returned his stare with twinkling eyes. 'You expect wrongly, Miss Barrington.' He looked down his patrician nose. 'Perhaps it would be better if I were to address you as Nurse.'

'Yes, Dr Winter.' The twinkle was so disconcerting that he looked away still frowning.

She had time to do the crossword puzzle before their flight was announced, leaving him to return to his reading.

She had a window seat on board and she was surprised to find that they were travelling first class, but pleased too, usually if she had to travel to a case, she was expected to use the cheapest way of getting there. She fastened her seat-belt and peered out of the window: it wasn't until they were airborne that she sat back in her seat.

'You've flown before?' asked Dr Winter. He didn't sound interested just polite, so she said that yes, once or twice, before turning her attention to the stewardess, who was explaining what they should all do in an emergency. And after that there was coffee and then lunch; and a very good one too, with a glass of white wine and coffee again. Isobel made a good meal, answered the doctor's occasional remarks politely and studied the booklet about Sweden offered for her perusal. A pity she wouldn't see more of the country, she thought, but she was lucky to have even a day in Stockholm; reading the tourist guide, there appeared to be a great deal to see.

There was someone waiting for them at the airport—a thickset man, very fair with level blue eyes and a calm face, leaning against a big Saab. He and Dr Winter greeted each other like old friends and when the doctor introduced Isobel, he took her hand in his large one and grinned at her. 'Janssen—Carl Janssen. It is a pleasure. We will go at once to my house and you will meet my wife Christina.'

He opened the car door and ushered her inside while Dr Winter got into the front seat. Isobel, who despite her placid nature had become a little chilled by his indifferent manner, felt more cheerful; Mr Janssen's friendly greeting had warmed her nicely. She made herself comfortable and watched the scenery.

It was beautiful. They were already approaching the city, which at first glance looked modern, but in the distance she could see a glimpse of water and there were a great many trees and parks. They slowed down as they neared the heart of the city and the streets became narrow and cobbled.

'This is Gamla Stan—the old town,' said Mr Janssen over one shoulder. 'We live here. It is quite the most beautiful part of Stockholm.'

He crossed a square: 'Look quickly—there is the old Royal Palace and Storkyrkan, our oldest church— you must pay it a visit.'

He swept the car into a labyrinth of narrow streets before she had had more than a glimpse, to stop and then turn into a narrow arched way between old houses. It opened on to a rectangular space filled with small gardens and ringed by old houses with a steeple roof and small windows and wrought iron balconies.

'This,' said Carl Janssen in a tone of deep satisfaction, 'is where we live.'

He opened the car door with a flourish and Isobel got out and looked around her. No one looking around them would have known that they were in the middle of a busy city. There was no one to be seen, although curtains blew at open windows and somewhere there was a baby crying and music. Between the high roofs she could see the thin steeple of a church and here and there in the gardens were lilacs, late blooming, and birds twittering in them.

'Heaven!' said Isobel.

Which earned her a pleased look from her host. 'Almost,' he agreed. 'But come in and meet Christina.'

He led the way between the little gardens to a small door and opened it. There was a steep staircase inside and Isobel, urged on by a friendly voice from above, climbed it. The girl at the top was about her own age, a big, fair-haired girl who took her hand as she reached the top and exclaimed: 'You are the nurse? Yes, my name is Christina.'

'Isobel.'

'That is pretty. Come in. Thomas, how wonderful to see you again!'

She flung her arms around the doctor's neck and kissed him warmly, and Isobel, standing back a little, thought how different he looked when he smiled like that. A pity he didn't do it more often. And discovering that his name was Thomas made him seem different.

Not that he was. He gave her a look which clearly was meant to keep her at a distance, said formally: 'Mr and Mrs Janssen are old friends of mine, Miss Barrington,' and stood aside politely so that she might walk into the narrow hallway.

It led to a roomy square hall from which doors led, presumably to the rest of the flat. Christina opened one of them and said gaily: 'Come in and sit, and we will have tea and then you shall see your rooms. Yours is the usual one, Thomas, and we have put Isobel in the corner room because from there she sees the garden below.'

She bustled round the large, comfortably furnished room, offering chairs, begging Isobel to take off her jacket, promising her that she should see the baby just as soon as he was awake. 'He is called Thomas, after this Thomas,' she laughed at Dr Winter, 'and we think that he is quite perfect!'

She went through another door to the kitchen and Carl started to talk about their trip. 'You have all the necessary papers?' he wanted to know. 'Without these there might be delays.' He smiled at Isobel. 'It is most sensible that you take Isobel with you, a good nurse may be most useful, especially as Mrs Olbinski is crippled.' He turned to Isobel. 'You are not nervous?'

'No, not at all—you mean because it's Poland? The Poles are friendly—they like us, though, don't they?'

'They are a most friendly people, and full of life.' He got up to help his wife with the tea tray and the talk centred upon Carl's work and where they intended to go for their summer holiday. 'We have a boat,' he told Isobel, 'and we sail a great deal on Lake Malaren and the Baltic. The islands offshore are beautiful and extend for miles—one can get lost among them.'

'You take little Thomas with you?'

'Of course. He is nine months old and a most easy baby.'

'You'll still be here when we get back?' Dr Winter asked casually.

'We go in three days' time, and if you are not back, but of course you will be, we will leave the key with our neighbours in the flat below. But you have ample time, even allowing for a day or so delay for one reason or another.' He looked at Dr Winter. 'She is well, your old nanny?'

'I telephoned last week—I'll ring again later if I may. She was very much looking forward to seeing us. And to coming home.'

'Well, you will stay as long as you wish to here,' declared Christina. 'Isobel, I will show you your room and when you have unpacked, come back here and we will talk some more.'

The room was charming, simply furnished, even a little austere, but there were flowers on a little table under the window and the gardens below with the old houses encircling them reminded Isobel of Hans Andersen's Fairy Tales. She looked at the plain pinewood bed with its checked duvet cover, and knew she was going to sleep soundly. It was a pity Dr Winter wasn't more friendly, but that was something which couldn't be helped. She had a shower, changed into a fresh blouse, did her face and hair and went back to the sitting room.

They ate in a tiny alcove off the sitting room after the baby had been fed and bathed and put to bed. The meal was typically Swedish, with a great dish of sprats, potatoes, onions and cream, which Carl translated as Janssen's Delight. This was followed by pancakes with jam, a great pot of coffee and Aquavit for the men.

The girls cleared the table, but once that was done, Isobel was amazed to see Dr Winter follow his friend into the splendidly equipped kitchen and shut the door.

'Thomas washes the dishes very well,' said Christina, and Isobel found herself faced with yet another aspect of the doctor which she hadn't even guessed at. Washing up, indeed! She wondered if the dignified manservant in London was aware of that and what he would have said.

She went to bed early, guessing that the other three might have things to talk about in which she had no part, and it wasn't until breakfast on the following morning that she learnt that Dr Winter had been unable to make his call; he had been told politely enough that there was no reply to the number he wanted. He was arguing the advantages of getting seats on the next flight to Gdansk when Carl said: 'Exactly what would be expected of you, Thomas. Keep to your plan and take the boat this evening,'

and Dr Winter had stared at him for a long minute
and then agreed.

'So that's settled,' said Christina. 'Thomas, you
will take Isobel to see something of Stockholm, and
when you come back I shall have made you the best
smörgasbörd table you ever tasted.'

So presently Isobel found herself going under the
archway, back into the narrow cobbled streets with
Dr Winter beside her. He had raised no objection to
accompanying her, neither had he shown any great
enthusiasm.

'Do you want to go to the shops?' he asked her as
they edged past a parked van and paused outside a
small antique shop.

'No, thank you. I should like to see St George and
the Dragon in the Storkyrkan, and the Riddarholm-
skyrkan, and then take a look at the lake. There won't
be time to go inside the palace, but if it wouldn't bore
you too much I should enjoy just walking through
some of the older streets.'

He glanced at his watch. 'Then we'd better begin
with St George,' was all he said.

He proved to be a good guide, for of course he had
been before and knew the names of the various build-
ings and how to get from one place to the next without getting lost. And he waited patiently while she
pottered round the churches, bought a few postcards
with the money he offered before she realised that
she would need to borrow some, and stood gazing at
the lake. It was a bright morning, but cool, and she

was glad of her jacket as she stood, trying to imagine what it must be like in the depths of winter.

'Have you been here in the winter?' she wanted to know.

'Oh, yes, several times. It's delightful. One needs to be able to ski and skate, of course.' He took it for granted that she could do neither of these things, and she saw no reason to correct him.

They had coffee at a small, crowded restaurant in one of the narrow paved streets, and she made no demur when he suggested that they should make their way back to the Janssens' flat. As they turned in under the arch once more, Dr Winter observed: 'One needs several days at least in order to see the best of Stockholm; there are some splendid museums if you're interested.'

'Well, yes, I am—and there's Millesgarden...all those statues—they're famous, aren't they? But I knew we couldn't have got there this morning.' She added hastily for fear he should take umbrage: 'Thank you very much for taking me round. I've enjoyed it enormously, it was most kind of you.'

They were standing outside the Janssens' door and it was very quiet and peaceful. He said harshly: 'No, it wasn't in the least kind, Miss Barrington. It never entered my head to take you sightseeing; I did it because Christina took it for granted that I would.'

Isobel opened the door. 'Well, I know that,' she said matter-of-factly.

After the smörgasbörd—a table weighted down with hot and cold dishes—the men went off together, leaving the girls to clear away, then put little Thomas into his pram and take him for a walk. They went through the narrow streets once more and came out by the water, finding plenty to talk about, although never once was Dr Winter mentioned.

The boat left in the early evening and after tea Isobel packed her case once more, said goodbye reluctantly enough, cheered by the thought that she would be back within the week, and went down to Carl's car.

The drive wasn't a long one, and once at the quay Isobel waited quietly while the two went off to see about their tickets, reappearing with a porter, and Carl then shook hands and dropped a friendly kiss on her cheek.

'We look forward to seeing you very soon, Isobel,' he told her. 'Even little Thomas will miss you.'

But not big Thomas, standing there, looking as impatient as good manners would allow.

The boat was large and comfortable. She had a splendid cabin with a small shower room and set about unpacking her uniform and hanging it up ready for their arrival in the morning. Dr Winter had handed her over to a stewardess with the suggestion that she should meet him in the restaurant once the ship had sailed—that meant an hour's time. She was ready long before then, and filled in the time reading the various leaflets she had collected about Gdansk and its harbour, Gdynia. They didn't tell her a great deal, but she studied them carefully. Once they were there, probably Dr Winter would have his hands full seeing to Mrs Olbinski's possessions and getting her to the ship, so she studied the map of those towns carefully too—one never knew.

He was waiting for her when she reached the restaurant, greeted her with the cool politeness she found so unnerving, and gave her a drink, and they dined presently—Swedish food, she was glad to discover; *kott bullarand* then fried boned herring and, once more, pancakes with jam. She didn't linger over their coffee and he didn't try and persuade her to stay. She wished him a cheerful goodnight and went back to her cabin, aware that he had been expecting her to ask any number of questions about the next day. In truth she had longed to do so, but had held her tongue. His opinion of her was already so low that she had no intention of making it lower. Let him tell her anything it was necessary for her to know. She fell asleep at once, rather pleased with herself.

CHAPTER TWO

ISOBEL WAS up early. She had slept well and now she was ready for her breakfast, but Dr Winter had suggested that they should meet in the restaurant at half past seven, and it was still only half past six. She rang, a shade apprehensively, for tea, then showered and dressed in her uniform and went on deck. They were close to land, she saw with a rising excitement, rather flat and wooded land with houses here and there. It was a pearly, still morning and chilly, and somehow London and home seemed a long way off. Isobel buttoned her navy gaberdine coat and wished she had put on her rather ugly nurse's blue felt hat. There wasn't any one else on deck and she started to walk along its length, to be confronted by Dr Winter coming out of a door.

His 'good morning' was polite and distant, and she was surprised when he fell into step beside her. 'I should perhaps mention,' he began casually, 'that there will probably be a delay in Mrs Olbinski's return. Carl told me there had been some trouble...' He didn't say what kind of trouble and Isobel didn't ask. She was surprised when he added: 'Are you a nervous person, Miss Barrington?'

She turned to face him. 'If you mean do I have

27

hysterics and screaming fits if things go wrong, no. But if a situation got out of hand, I would probably behave like most women and scream for help.'

He said seriously: 'I must ask you not to do that; a calm, serene front is important.'

She started walking again. 'Is there something you should have told me before we left England?' she asked in a voice which she managed to keep calm.

'Certainly not, Miss Barrington. I must remind you merely that each country has its own laws. Mrs Olbinski's husband was unfortunately a dissident, so naturally they may be somewhat more strict...'

She stopped again and eyed him thoughtfully. 'You have got all the permits?' she asked.

'Of course. I'm only saying that because of her circumstances there may be some delay.' He frowned. 'We might as well go and have our breakfast.'

'Oh, good—I'm hungry. But before we go, where exactly are we now?'

'Coming into Gdynia, which is the port of Gdansk. Mrs Olbinski lives in the old town of Gdansk and you'll have a chance to see it.'

Isobel scanned the nearing coastline. 'Oh, good— Poland isn't a place I'm likely to come to again. Do they speak English?'

'A great many do, but I doubt if you'll have time to go sightseeing.'

She felt snubbed. Did he really think she would disappear the moment they landed, intent on enjoying herself? Her splendid appetite had had the edge taken off it.

Going through Customs took a good deal of time; she had to admire Dr Winter's calm patience in the face of the courteous questioning that went on at some length. When finally they were free to go, one of the officials apologised for the delay with the utmost politeness and the doctor waived the apologies with an equal politeness. As they got into the taxi he said: 'Sorry about that; understandably I had to give my reasons for our visit and they had to be checked.'

He told the driver where to go. 'There's nothing much to see here, but you'll find Gdansk interesting, I believe.'

They drove through a dock area which might have been anywhere in the world and presently came to Gdansk, where the taxi stopped before an enormous gateway, its centre arch opening into a wide paved street.

'This is where we walk,' observed Dr Winter, and got out.

He wasted no time in giving more than a glance at the enormous edifice before them but took her arm and walked her briskly through the archway and into the street beyond. It was a splendid sight, lined with Renaissance houses, many of them with small shops at street level. Isobel, going along a great deal faster than she wished, did her best to look everywhere at once and as they reached a square at the end of the street asked in a voice which demanded an answer.

'Is that the Town Hall we've just passed? And is that the Golden House I read about? And this fountain in the centre…?'

The doctor didn't pause in his walk. 'Miss Barrington, may I remind you that you're here for one purpose only; sightseeing is quite another matter.'

'If this is sightseeing then I'm a Dutchman,' declared Isobel roundly, 'and I only asked you a question!'

He looked at her, trotting along beside him, very sober in her uniform, and said harshly: 'If you remember, Miss Barrington, I said at the time of your interview that you weren't suitable.'

Unanswerable. They were going through another enormous gate with water beyond and warehouses on the opposite bank. But Dr Winter turned left, making his way along the busy street bordering the water, left again into a narrow street lined with lovely old houses. Half way down he stopped before an arched door and rang one of the many bells on the wall. To Isobel's surprise he turned to look at her. 'The city was in ruins after the last war. The Poles rebuilt it, brick by brick, many of them original, the rest so skilfully done that it's hard to detect the one from the other.' He then turned his back on her as the door opened, revealing a short narrow hall and a staircase beyond. 'Third floor,' he told her over his shoulder, and began to mount.

Isobel followed perforce, liking her surroundings very much; the wooden stairway, the small circular landings, the two solid wooden doors on each of these. On the third floor one of the doors was open. The doctor went in without hesitation, and Isobel, a little breathless, followed him.

The door opened on to a tiny vestibule with two doors and they stood open too. The doctor unhesitatingly went through the left-hand one, with Isobel so close on his heels that she almost overbalanced when he halted abruptly.

The room was small, nicely furnished and far too warm. The table in the centre of the room was polished to a high gloss and so were the chairs. The wooden floor shone with polish too and the curtains at the windows, although limp with age, were spotless. Isobel registered vaguely that the room looked bare before turning her attention to the old lady sitting in a chair whose tapestry was threadbare with age. She was a very small lady with bright bootbutton eyes, white hair strained back into a knob, and wearing a black dress covered by a cotton pinafore.

She said in a surprisingly strong voice, 'Mr Thomas...' She glanced at the small carved wooden clock on the mantelpiece. 'Punctual, I see. You always were as a little boy.' Her eyes darted to Isobel. 'And who is this?'

Dr Winter bent and kissed and hugged her gently. 'Hullo, Nanny. Nice to see you again. This is Nurse Barrington, I brought her along to give you a hand.'

Mrs Olbinski pushed her specs up her nose and

stared at Isobel through them. 'H'm—rather small. Come here, young lady, so I can see you properly.'

Isobel did as she was asked. Old people said strange things sometimes, just as though one wasn't there, listening, but she didn't mind; probably she would do the same one day. 'How do you do?' she asked politely.

'Almost plain,' commented the old lady to no one in particular, 'but nice eyes and a nice smile too!' She bristled suddenly. 'Not that I need a nurse; I'm quite able to get around on my own...'

'Well, of course you are.' Isobel had never heard the doctor speak in such a soft, coaxing voice. 'I asked her to come for purely selfish reasons; there'll be people to see and so on, and I didn't want the worry of leaving you while I dealt with them.'

He had struck the right note. Nanny nodded in agreement. 'When do we leave?' she asked.

'By this evening's ferry, my dear. Have you packed?'

'There are still one or two things, Mr Thomas. I daresay this young lady will help me?'

'Of course, Mrs Olbinski—and my name is Isobel.'

'Now that's a good name, and one I've always liked. You can go into the kitchen and make the coffee, while I hear all the news.'

Isobel was in the minute kitchen, stealthily opening cupboards, looking for things, when she heard several pairs of feet coming up the stairs. The door wasn't quite shut, and she had no hesitation in going and

standing as close to it as she could get. She didn't
dare look round the door's edge, but she judged the
feet to be either policemen or soldiers because of the
hefty boots.

Soldiers. A rather nice voice, speaking excellent
English, pointing out with regret that a final paper
which was needed by Mrs Olbinski had not yet arrived. It was therefore necessary that she should stay
until it did.

'And when will that be?' The doctor's voice
sounded friendly, unhurried and not in the least put
out.

'Tomorrow—the day following that at the latest.
We deeply regret any inconvenience.'

'I quite understand that it is unavoidable and not
of your making.' There was a short silence. 'I will
get rooms for myself and the nurse I have brought
with me at the Orbis Monopol. Mrs Olbinski will prefer to stay here, I expect.'

There was the faintest question in his voice.

'Of course, she will be perfectly all right, Dr Winter. As soon as the papers come, I will let you know
so that you may complete your plans.'

The goodbyes sounded friendly enough—and why
not? Isobel reasoned. The Poles and the English liked
each other; whoever it was who had just gone had
had a delightful voice... She wasn't quite quick
enough at getting away from the door; she found the
doctor's austere good looks within inches of her head.
'Next time you eavesdrop, young lady, control your

breathing—you sounded like an overwrought female from an early Victorian novel.' He looked round the kitchen. 'Isn't the coffee ready yet?'

'No, it's not, and I wish someone would explain...'

'But there's nothing to explain. As you must know, anyone leaving the country must have their papers in order; Nanny's are not quite completed, that is all. You should be delighted; we shall have a day for sightseeing.'

She looked at him thoughtfully. 'Would you like me to stay here with Mrs Olbinski?'

He smiled for the first time, so nicely that she found herself almost liking him. 'That's very thoughtful of you, but there's no need. You shall enjoy the comfort of the best hotel here and tomorrow we'll take Nanny sightseeing; I daresay she'll be glad to say goodbye to as many places as possible; she hasn't had the opportunity, you see.'

The kettle boiled and Isobel poured the water into the enamel coffee pot she had found in one of the cupboards, set it on the tray with the cups and saucers off the shelf above the stove, and handed the doctor the tray. She smiled very faintly at the look of surprise as he took it. She didn't think he was a selfish man, merely one who had never had to fend for himself. Too clever, no doubt, with his splendid nose buried in books or people's insides while others ministered to his mundane wants.

Mrs Olbinski was sitting in her chair, looking impatient. 'You took a long time,' she observed tartly.

'I have always been under the impression that nurses are able to do everything anywhere at any time.' She sniffed: 'Not that I believe it for one moment.'

'Well, no I shouldn't think you would, because that's a load of nonsense,' said Isobel forthrightly. 'I suppose we're trained to do some things others might not be able to do, but that's all—besides, this is a foreign land to me and your kitchen isn't quite the same.' She added hastily: 'Though it's charming and very cosy.'

Mrs Olbinski accepted her coffee and took a sip. 'The coffee isn't bad,' she conceded, 'and you seem a sensible young woman. Where did Mr Thomas find you?'

Isobel didn't look at the doctor, looming on the other side of the little dark table. 'Dr Winter asked an agency to send him a nurse,' she explained in a colourless voice. 'It was me or no one.'

Dr Winter made an impatient movement and she waited for him to say something, but he didn't, so she went on: 'It might make your journey a little easier if I give you a hand from time to time, just while Dr Winter sees to papers and passports and things…'

'You don't look very strong. Why do you keep saying Dr Winter in that fashion?'

Isobel sighed and went red as Dr Winter said repressively: 'Miss Barrington and I…' he stopped and began again. 'We've only recently met, Nanny.'

Nanny made a sound which sounded like Faugh! and then Phish! 'Well, I shall call her Isobel; it's a pretty name even if she isn't a pretty girl. And you can do the same, Mr Thomas, because you must be old enough to be her father. I'll have some more coffee.'

She took no notice of the doctor's remote annoyance but sat back comfortably in her chair. 'If we're to be here for another day, perhaps you'd take me to Oliwa; there'll be organ recitals in the afternoons now that it's summer, and I should dearly love to hear one before I go.'

Her old voice crumbled and the doctor said quickly: 'What a splendid idea, Nanny. I'll rent a car and we'll drive over there tomorrow—how about a quick look at Sopot as well?'

'Oh, I'd love that above all things—we used to go there in the summer...' She launched into a recital of her life while her husband had been alive, until Dr Winter interrupted her gently: 'Well, you shall see as much as possible, but in the meantime I think you might let Nurse... Isobel finish your packing, don't you?' He got up. 'Suppose I leave you for an hour while I see about a car and our rooms at the hotel?'

He stooped and picked her up out of her chair and carried her through the second door into a small bedroom. He paused on the threshold—and no wonder; there wasn't an inch of space, there were boxes, bundles and an old trunk taking up every available corner. Isobel cleared a pile of books off a chair, remarking comfortably: 'If you'll tell me what has to be done, I'll do it, Mrs Olbinski.'

'A sensible girl,' observed that lady succinctly. 'All this must go with me.'

Dr Winter was edging round the room looking at its contents. He said with gentle firmness: 'I'm afraid that you won't be allowed to take more than the clothing you're wearing and your most treasured possessions. No money, of course. Small stuff which will go into a suitase, or a well tied cardboard box.' He went to the door. 'I'll be back presently.'

Isobel took off her coat and hat. 'Men!' declared Mrs Olbinski pettishly. 'They're all alike, so quick to tell us of the unpleasant tasks they want done, and just as quick to go away until they're completed.' She darted a look at Isobel. 'But Mr Thomas is a good man, make no mistake, my dear—too clever, of course, with his head in his books and always working, never finding the time to get himself a wife and children.'

Isobel murmured politely, her mind occupied solely with the problem of how to pack a quart into a pint bottle—something, a great many things, would have to be discarded.

'What will you wear to travel in?' she asked. A question which led to a long discussion as to the merits of a shabby winter coat or an equally shabby raincoat. They settled on the coat, a weary felt hat to go with it, a dark dress, gloves and shoes, and Isobel hung them thankfully in the corner cupboard. Underclothes were quickly dealt with, largely because there were not many; and that left mounds of small bits and pieces, all of which Mrs Olbinski declared were vital to her future life in England. Isobel didn't say much, merely sorted family photos, a few trinkets, and a handful of small ornaments from the old scarves, ribbons, bits of lace and books. These she packed before going in search of something in which to put a few, at least, of the books.

She found a shopping basket in the kitchen and then patiently brought over Mrs Olbinski's remaining treasures so that she could decide which must be left behind. This took time too, but at last it was done, and Isobel suggested tentatively that there might be someone her companion knew who might be glad to have the remainder of the books and vases and clothes.

The old lady brightened. 'Go and knock on the door below, Isobel—there's a pleasant woman living there; she might be glad of these things since I'm not to be allowed to keep them.' She added crossly: 'Why doesn't Mr Thomas come back? He's doing nothing to help.'

Too true, thought Isobel, wrestling with the lady downstairs' valiant attempts to speak English. Signs and smiles and a few urgent tugs to an elderly arm did the trick at last; they went back upstairs together and Isobel left Mrs Olbinski to explain to her friend, who was so pleased with the arrangement that Isobel felt near to tears; how poor they must be, she thought, to be so glad with what were no more than clothes fit for the jumble. When she could get a word in edge-

ways she suggested that once Mrs Olbinski had gone,
the lady might like to come back and collect the bed-
clothes and what food there was left. And that wasn't
much—she had had a look. She had just ushered the
delighted lady back to her own flat, deposited her new
possessions in the sitting-room and wished her goodbye when the street door below opened. It could be
anyone, it could be Dr Winter; she didn't wait to find
out, but skipped upstairs once more to her charge.

It was Dr Winter, calm and unhurried and far too
elegant for his surroundings. 'There you are,' declared
Isobel, quite forgetting her place. 'Just nicely back
when all the work is done!'

He chose to misunderstand her. 'Oh, splendid. I
have rooms at the hotel and there's a car at the end
of the street. I'm taking you out to lunch, Nanny, and
since we have time on our hands, we'll take a short
drive this afternoon.'

'I can't go like this!' The old lady was querulous;
getting tired.

'If you wait a few minutes, I'll help Mrs Olbinski
to put on her things,' suggested Isobel, and when he
had gone, fetched the clothes from the cupboard and
set about helping the old lady, wondering how she
had managed in the lonely months since her husband's death, with her poor twisted hands and frail
bent body. It took a little time, but the doctor made
no comment when she called to him that they were
ready. He picked up the old lady, reminded Isobel to
lock the door behind them, and went down the narrow

stairs. Once on the pavement they each took an arm,
and made a slow painful progress to the car where
the doctor set Mrs Olbinski in the seat beside his and
bade Isobel get in the back. It was a small car and he
looked out of place driving it.

The hotel was large and once Mrs Olbinski was
comfortably settled with the doctor, Isobel was shown
to her room, large and well furnished and with a
shower room next door. She unpacked her case, did
her face and hair and went downstairs again. It was,
of course, a pity they couldn't return to Stockholm at
once, but on the other hand it would be a golden
opportunity to get even a glimpse of Gdansk. She
looked forward to their promised outing with all the
pleasure of a child.

They lunched presently in a stylish restaurant, half
empty, for as the waiter told them, the summer season
had barely started. The meal was wholly Polish—hot
beet soup, crayfish, pork knuckle with horseradish
sauce, followed by ices. Isobel enjoyed it all, and so,
she noticed, did Mrs Olbinski.

They set off once lunch was finished, with the old
lady quite excited now. They were to go to Sopot, a
seaside resort only a few miles away and which she
had known very well in earlier days. 'We went each
year for our holiday here; there was a small hotel,
quite near the Grand Orbis Hotel, and we would
watch the people staying there in the evening, going
in and out in their evening dress,' she sighed. 'Such
a beautiful place!'

Very beautiful agreed Isobel, but almost deserted. They drove slowly about its streets; there were few people about and the shop windows looked almost empty, and at length they turned towards the sea and parked the car in a long avenue of trees. The sense of solitude was enhanced by the wide beach, quite deserted too, and the chilly grey of the Baltic beyond. 'We'll walk nearer so you can have a better view. Nanny will be all right and we can see her easily enough.'

There was a narrow concrete bridge crossing the sands, reached by a spiral staircase. It was a minute's walk away and Isobel ran up it ahead of the doctor to stand and admire the coast line stretching away on either side of her. 'This must be lovely on a warm summer's day,' she said, 'and with lots of people here.' She started to walk beside him towards the stairs at its other end. 'Where are all the people?' she wanted to know.

'The country is under martial law,' he reminded her. 'There's little money for holidays, and still less for food; I daresay tourists from other countries will come here when it's high summer.'

'It's very sad—your nanny must find it sad too.'

'She has her happy memories. We'll find somewhere for tea and then drive along the coast. In Poland the main meal in a normal household is eaten about four o'clock, but we should be able to get tea or coffee and then have dinner at the hotel before taking Nanny back. You'll be good enough to help her to bed and leave everything at hand.'

They were walking back to the car across the path built on the sand.

'Wouldn't you like me to sleep there tonight?' asked Isobel. 'I'll be quite comfortable...'

'There's no need for that. You'll go to her after breakfast—I'll drive you there before going to check her papers—they may arrive by then.'

'Suppose they don't?'

'Then we'll spend another day here.'

They had coffee in a small café in the town and the owner pulled up a chair, delighted to air his English. He was a middle-aged man, with dark eyes and full of wry humour. They stayed quite a while, so that their drive along the coast wasn't as lengthy as Isobel had hoped, all the same she listened to Mrs Olbinski's titbits of information about the country around them and looked at houses and churches and old castles with all the zeal of a tourist.

They had dinner very soon after they got back to the hotel—soup again, grilled beef and dumplings and an ice. Dr Winter drank vodka, which Isobel prudently refused, although she did drink the beer he offered her. Nanny had vodka too, that and the good food and unexpected treat of a drive that afternoon had rendered her nicely sleepy. They took her back to her flat and the doctor waited while Isobel helped her to bed, tidying up afterwards and leaving coffee ready for the morning.

'You're a good girl,' declared Mrs Olbinski, when she went to say goodnight. 'How old are you?'

'Twenty-five, Mrs Olbinski.'

Nanny gave a chuckle. 'I shall be eighty in six weeks' time,' she declared. 'I'll have a proper birthday too with a cake and presents.'

Isobel and Dr Winter went back to the hotel in silence, only when they had gained the foyer did he bid her goodnight. 'Breakfast at half past eight, Nurse,' he reminded her, 'and afterwards we'll go immediately to Mrs Olbinski's flat.'

She didn't ask questions; there was no point, since she was sure that he wouldn't answer them. She went up to her room, had a shower, washed her hair and went to bed.

She woke early to a grey morning and the sound of early traffic in the street below. It was barely seven o'clock, a whole one and a half hours before she could go to breakfast, and she was wide awake and longing for a cup of tea. She went to peer out of the window and then on impulse, got dressed; there was still more than an hour to breakfast, she would explore a little, it would pass the time, and she had little hope of that meal being earlier if the doctor had said half past eight, then that was the time at which they would breakfast—not a minute sooner, not a minute later; she knew him well enough to know that. He would be a strict father, she mused, brushing her mousey hair, but kind and gentle. And why should I suppose that? she enquired of her neat reflection, he's never been either of those things to me. She pulled a childish face in the mirror, put on her coat and hat and left the room, locking the door carefully behind her.

There was a woman cleaning the corridor and a porter behind the reception desk in the foyer. Both of them replied to her good morning and the porter gave her a questioning look so that she said: 'I'm going for a short walk,' and smiled at him as she reached the big swing door.

Before she could open it, Dr Winter came in from outside, took her by the elbow and marched her back to the foyer.

'Where the hell do you think you're going?' he asked in a voice so harsh and so unlike his usual bland coolness that all Isobel could do was gape at him.

Presently she managed: 'Only going for a walk.'

'Going for a walk,' he mimicked mockingly. 'Of course you can speak Polish, know your way around Gdansk and have your passport with you, not to mention enough money for a taxi back if you should get lost.'

She said reasonably: 'I was only going a little way—close to the hotel, and you have no need to be so nasty about it, Dr Winter.'

She peered up into his angry face and saw that it was grey with fatigue and needed a shave. 'And where have you been?' she asked with disconcerting candour. 'You're cross and tired and you haven't shaved... Out all night?' She kept her pleasant voice low. 'At Mrs Olbinski's flat? She's ill?'

He shook his head. 'No, your eyes are too sharp, Nurse, and it's just my confounded luck to meet you...'

'There was a curfew.' She raised troubled eyes to meet his dark ones.

'Lifted half an hour since. I didn't like the idea of leaving Nanny alone.' And at her look: 'Oh, you were safe enough, the porter knew where I was; he's a friend of hers anyway, he promised to keep an eye on you.'

He didn't look angry any more, only faintly amused and impatient.

'And now, if you've finished your questioning, I'll have a shower and shave and join you for breakfast.' He caught her arm again. 'You'll oblige me by staying in your room until I come for you, and I'd like your promise on that.'

'I never heard such nonsense!' said Isobel impatiently. 'You've just said the curfew is over.'

'Your promise,' he insisted in a voice she didn't much like the sound of.

'Oh, very well.' She went with him up the stairs and when he took her key and opened her door, went past him without a word, only at the last minute she whizzed round and held out her hand.

Dr Winter put the key into it. He said softly: 'You are, after all, my responsibility until we're back in England.'

They breakfasted in a comfortable silence, broken only by polite requests to pass the salt, the toast or whatever. Dr Winter's face had lost its greyness; he was freshly shaved, impeccably dressed and very calm. Isobel, taking a quick peep, asked when she should go to Mrs Olbinski.

'We'll go together,' he told her, 'and while you're helping her to dress I'll go and see if her papers are in order. If so we can leave on the evening boat.'

Isobel had just coaxed Mrs Olbinski into the last of her garments when he returned to say that there would be no papers until the following morning. 'So we may as well spend the day sightseeing,' he finished. 'Where would you like to go, Nanny?'

'Oliwa,' she said at once, 'to listen to the organ recital—it's at twelve noon, I believe.'

They had coffee first in the hotel coffee room and then got into the car and drove the few miles to Oliwa. The Cathedral was magnificent—twelfth century, with Renaissance Baroque and Rococo added from time to time. The doctor parked the car and they began the slow progress to its entrance with Mrs Olbinski in the middle, insisting that she would rather die than be carried. The interior was splendid, with a high vaulted roof, painted with stars and hung with the Polish flag and with old-fashioned pews, already well-filled. They found seats near the back, and presently the recital started with a disembodied voice explaining in English what music would be played and the history of the Cathedral, ending with the advice to turn round and look at the organ at the back of the Cathedral when the organist broke into particularly loud music. Isobel, with Mrs Olbinski's old hand in hers, only half listened. This was the real Poland, she thought, here in church, with the flag hanging on either side of the chancel and the quiet people sitting in the pews around her. The organ began then and she sat for half an hour, as still as a mouse, listening until the organist suddenly broke into a tremendous volume of sound. It was Dr Winter who leaned across Mrs Olbinski and touched her arm. 'Look behind you,' he said softly.

The organ, a massive eighteenth-century instrument, had come alive. The figures carved on it, angels with harps, trumpets, violins and flutes, were moving with the music, playing their instruments. The doctor's hand was still on her arm; she clutched it tightly and only when the music finally faded did she let it go, dropping it like a hot coal when she realised she had been clinging to it. 'So sorry,' she whispered, very pink, and was hardly reassured by his inscrutable face.

They went back to Gdansk for lunch, eating it at the Pod Wieza restaurant, and when they had finished, the doctor left them there, saying he would be back presently.

He was back within half an hour, during which time Isobel and Mrs Olbinski had had several cups of coffee and a good gossip. 'We can leave this evening,' he told them. He glanced at his watch. 'We'll go back to the hotel and get our things and pay the bill, then go to your place, Nanny. From there we can go down to the quay.'

Mrs Olbinski tried not to show her excitement but her old hands shook. 'You're sure, Mr Thomas? Everything's in order?'

'Yes, Nanny, we'll have you home in a couple of days now.' He smiled at her gently and took out a handkerchief and wiped her eyes for her. Oh, dear, thought Isobel; he is so nice when he's not being absolutely abominable!

Nice he might be to Nanny, but he allowed none of his finer feelings to show where Isobel was concerned. In businesslike tones he told her what had to be done, and she was kept busy, once they reached the old lady's rooms, parcelling up the things, which were to go to her neighbour, making tea for the three of them, and packing a small bag with essentials for the journey for both herself and Mrs Olbinski.

After tea the doctor took back the hired car, found a taxi and started on the slow business of loading Nanny and her few possessions into it. The old lady was fretful from excitement and tiredness by now and hindered every move. It was with a sigh of relief that Isobel saw the ferry at last, and even then she wasn't completely happy until they were actually stepping off the gangway on to the ship. Nanny was in tears again. She had, after all, lived in Poland for a long time and was leaving a life she had loved until the more recent years. Isobel coaxed her down to their cabin, got her undressed and into one of the bunks, and rang the bell for the stewardess. A large cheerful Swedish woman came at once; listening sympathetically she promised a light supper within the hour. Isobel unpacked the few things they needed for the night, talked Mrs Olbinski into a quiet frame of mind and when the supper came, sat down. Dr Winter hadn't said anything about her own meal and she wasn't sure if she wasn't supposed to have it in the cabin too. She was trying to decide what to do next when he knocked on the door and came in.

He enquired after Nanny's wellbeing and assured her that the stewardess would come the moment she was rung for, and invited Isobel with cold courtesy to join him at dinner. 'We'll go now and have a drink,' he concluded without giving her a chance to say anything.

So she followed him to the deck above, drank the sherry he invited her to have and sat down to dinner. He had little to say for himself, and she was glad of that; such a lot had happened in the last two days, she wanted to think about them.

However, over coffee he said suddenly: 'I think we may have to stay a couple of days in Stockholm,' and at her look of delight, added dryly: 'Not for sightseeing. Nanny is worn out and I'm not happy about continuing our journey until she has had a good rest.'

Isobel blushed. 'Yes, of course—she's been marvellous. It must have been pretty nerve-racking for her. I'll keep her in bed and get her to rest as much as possible.' She added: 'She won't like it.'

He passed his cup for more coffee. 'That's your business, Nurse. At least she likes you and will probably do as you ask.'

She said cheerfully: 'Let's hope so, I'll do my best, Dr Winter.' She put her cup down. 'Thank you for my dinner—I'm going back to the cabin now. I'll see that Mrs Olbinski is ready by the time we get to Stockholm—she can have her breakfast early and that will give us plenty of time.'

'You'll breakfast here?'

She said matter-of-factly: 'No, thanks, I'll have coffee and something when Mrs Olbinski does. Where are we to meet you in the morning?'

'I'll come for you.' He got up as she prepared to leave. 'Goodnight, Nurse.'

She gave him a friendly nod. 'Goodnight, Dr Winter.'

He didn't sit down again, but stood watching her neat figure as she threaded her way past the tables. If she had turned round she would have been surprised indeed to see that he was smiling.

CHAPTER THREE

MRS OLBINSKI slept like a child, and like a child,
woke early, so that there was ample time to help her
dress after their coffee and rolls. By the time the
docks were closing in on them they were both ready,
so that when Dr Winter tapped on their door they
were able to go with him without the smallest hitch.

It was a fine morning with a fresh breeze blowing
from the Baltic, so that Mrs Olbinski shivered a little
as Isobel helped her down the gangway with the doctor in front holding the old lady's hand—'Like a
crab,' chortled Nanny, and allowed herself to be
helped towards the Customs shed and the Passport
office. There was a short delay while her papers were
examined by one man, given to another to read and
then handed back again, but her passport was stamped
and the three of them made their slow progress to the
waiting taxis. To Isobel's questioning look, the doctor
said: 'No, Carl won't be here to meet us. We're going
straight to their flat, although I rather fancy we shall
have missed them by a couple of hours—they were
going on holiday if you remember.'

The flat was empty when they reached it. Dr Winter
carried Nanny up the stairs, took the door key from
under the mat, and went inside. There was a note for

him, and while Isobel saw to Mrs Olbinski, he read it, chuckling a good deal. 'That's all right,' he said at length, 'we may stay here as long as we wish.' He looked at the old lady with an apparently careless eye.

'Tired, my dear? How about bed for a while? Coffee first, though.'

Which was Isobel's cue, she supposed, to go into the splendid little kitchen and make it. When she got back the doctor was lying back in a chair with his eyes closed and Mrs Olbinski was snoring gently. He opened his eyes as she set the tray on the table and got up to fetch his coffee.

'Have your coffee, Isobel, then we'll wake her and get her to bed. I think it likely that we'll stay here for rather more than two days.' He paused. 'Why do you look so dumbfounded? I'd already said it was likely…'

'You called me Isobel.'

His eyebrows rose. 'Do you object? Since we're to be in each other's company for the next few days.'

'I don't mind in the least, Dr Winter.' She spoke in her usual matter-of-fact voice, and wondered what would happen if she called him Thomas. Probably he would explode. She smiled at the idea and he asked sharply: 'Why are you smiling?'

She said 'nothing' so firmly that it sounded almost true.

Mrs Olbinski wakened a few minutes later, declaring that she hadn't been to sleep, only shut her eyes; all the same, when she had drunk her coffee she went willingly enough with Isobel and allowed herself to be helped into her nightgown and settled in bed. She said rather fretfully: 'I haven't thanked Mr Thomas—whatever must he think of me? And I'm so grateful…it will be nice to be looked after.' She put out a hand and caught Isobel's. 'You're a dear child, Isobel, looking after a tiresome old woman who can't even remember to say thank you.'

'Hush now,' said Isobel, her pleasant voice gentle. 'You're tired and you've had a lot to do in the last day or so, I don't think Th… Dr Winter expects you to thank him until you're quite yourself again. If you have a good nap now, how about him coming here and having a cup of tea with you later on, then there'll be time to thank him properly.' She popped the elderly hand under the blanket. 'I'm sure he's tired too…all those papers…'

'It must have taken him months, and then that delay.' The old voice trembled. 'I thought just for a while that I wouldn't be able to come with you.'

'But everything turned out perfectly all right, didn't it?'

She went back to the sitting room once she was sure that Mrs Olbinski was asleep and found Dr Winter stretched out on the enormous sofa; he was snoring gently.

She collected the coffee cups soundlessly, bore them off to the kitchen and then went and sat down by the window. The garden below was charming; she spent some time admiring it and then, since the doctor showed no signs of waking, crept away to the kitchen to open cupboards and peer inside. Sooner or later, he would wake up and want a meal, it would help if she had some idea of what there was to cook. Soup for Nanny—that was easy; there was a row of tins, the wrappers illustrating their contents. In the freezer there was food in abundance, the only thing was that it was all wrapped and neatly labelled in Swedish. As soon as the doctor woke up she would ask him to go shopping. Thank heaven there were potatoes in plenty. She peeled some and set them on the stove ready to cook later on, then she sat down at the kitchen table and made a list of things to buy—too bad if the shops shut at noon; it was almost that already, and as far as she could remember there weren't many shops close by, only antique dealers and smart boutiques. The list grew alarmingly. She was doing her best to cut it down to a reasonable length when the doctor joined her.

Predictably he asked: 'Lunch?'

She eyed him severely. 'If you would be good enough to look in the freezer and tell me what's in all those packs, I can thaw something for this evening,' she told him. 'As for lunch—we need bread, milk and something to go on the bread. There's soup for Mrs Olbinski if she should wake.'

'My poor Isobel, left to wrestle with household problems while I take my ease!' He opened the freezer door and examined several packs. 'Chops,' he told her, and put them on the table, 'lamb chops. And

I'll go out now and get what you need—we'd better have sandwiches.'

At the door he turned to look at her. 'Can you cook?'

'Yes—not Cordon Bleu, just plain cooking.'

'I see I have a treasure in you—nurse, companion to the elderly, excellent coffee maker, Girl Friday—oh, and a good plain cook...'

She went slowly red under his bland look and he made it worse by adding: 'Nothing personal intended, Isobel.'

There was no reason why she should mind so much, she told herself as she laid the kitchen table and found cups and saucers and plates, and then, because he wasn't back, she went along to the bedroom she had had before and did her hair and tidied herself. Perhaps now that they were back in Stockholm she could wear her own clothes again; she must remember to ask.

For a bachelor who, from her visit to his house, wasn't in the habit of doing the shopping, he had done very well—rolls and croissants, a plastic container with a delicious-looking salad of seafood, mushrooms and tomatoes, cheese and ham, fruit and a bottle of wine. Dr Winter laid them neatly on the table, took a roll and bit into it. 'I'll go out again when we've eaten and get whatever you want to cook for this evening. Make a list, will you?'

'Well, I have, but perhaps you'll think it's too much... There are the lamb chops, and I've got potatoes—if you got things for a salad and celery, I'll braise that, and if you like onions I could do Lyonnaise potatoes. I don't know if there's any rhubarb, if not apples will do, and I'll make a pie—we'll need some cream. I don't know the cheeses they sell here, but if you could get a little of several sorts; I found some crackers in the cupboard, and there's plenty of butter.'

She glanced up from her list and found him looking at her so intently that she said: 'Oh, is there something you don't like? I can easily alter it, it was just a rough idea…'

'It sounds marvellous, and if that's a rough idea I do hope I'm there when you really put your mind to it.' He smiled at her, not the usual cold smile he offered her, but a warm friendly grin. 'Who taught you to cook?' he asked.

'My mother.' She was cutting the rolls in half and buttering them.

'Have you brothers and sisters—a father?'

He was sitting on a chair, round the wrong way so that his arms rested along its back.

'A brother. My father died some years ago.' She would have liked to have talked to him about her family, but if she did she had no doubt that after a minute he would look faintly bored. She added rapidly: 'Would you like cheese in the rolls, or do I put this salad in them?'

'It's called *vastkustsallad*, it'll be easier to manage

on plates.' He sighed gently. 'Our relationship is hardly a happy one, is it, Isobel?'

Her eyes flew to his face. 'But we haven't got a relationship, Dr Winter. I'm a nurse hired to help you with Mrs Olbinski—and you only hired me because there was no one else.' She spoke in her usual quiet friendly fashion, stating a fact without rancour.

He didn't answer but set about opening the wine, and she finished filling the rolls. 'I'll just look in on Mrs Olbinski, if she's awake she might like some soup.'

Nanny was sleeping deeply. Isobel went back to the kitchen and invited the doctor to his lunch. 'I hope you don't mind having it in here, just this once...'

He sat down opposite her, looming from his side of the table.

'You sound as though you imagine I never have eaten in a kitchen before.'

'Well, I don't suppose you do often, do you? You live in a very grand house.'

'My home, Isobel, and it happens to have a very pleasant kitchen. Will you try some of this salad, it's famous in these parts.'

She made coffee presently and over it he said: 'I have to go out this afternoon. I'll do your shopping first, though. You'll be all right here?'

'Yes, of course. Is there anything I ought to know about Mrs Olbinski?'

'Only that her heart isn't too good—I examined her when I was at her flat. There's very little to be done,

I'm afraid—we'll keep her in bed for two days at least before we go back to England. She can get up if she wants to for an hour or so, but otherwise strict bed rest. Have you all you want for her?'

'I think so, thank you.' Isobel got up. 'I'll wash up. Do you mind if I get back into my other clothes?'

His cool look appraised her. 'Not in the least—wear whatever you like.' His tone implied that she could drape herself in a sack if she wanted to.

She stacked the dishes with a noiseless emphasis more telling than smashing plates. He was horrid, rude and thoughtless and always telling her what had to be done; it would do him good to do a few chores for himself!

Disconcerting therefore when he went to the sink and washed up.

She was heating some soup for Mrs Olbinski who had wakened feeling waspish, when he came back with the groceries. Then he unpacked them on to the kitchen table, enquired after the old lady, spent a few minutes with her and let himself out of the flat again. And all without more than a hullo and goodbye. But why should I care? she asked the kitchen at large as she was preparing an appetising snack for her patient.

Mrs Olbinski went back to sleep presently and Isobel went into the sitting room and picked up a magazine. She couldn't understand a word of it, but the pictures were interesting. The doctor wasn't back by the time she decided to make tea. She would have liked a long hot bath and to have washed her hair and changed her skirt and top, but he'd left her in charge and supposing the phone rang or someone called or Mrs Olbinski wanted her? She drank her tea and went along to see how the old lady fared. She was still sleeping, but lightly now. Isobel crept around putting out clean clothes, fetching her own soap, clean towels and a brush and comb and in a little while, when Mrs Olbinski woke once more, she made fresh tea, found biscuits and then when the old lady had had her tea, set about her toilet. It was remarkable what a difference a fresh nightie, a wash with scented soap and a well brushed head did to improve matters. Mrs Olbinski, sitting up against comfortable pillows, smiled contentedly. 'Well, I must say I feel better for that,' she conceded, 'and I do believe I could eat a little supper presently. Where is Mr Thomas?'

'He's here, just got back,' said the doctor, coming down the hall and into her room. 'And what a sight for sore eyes, Nanny—you don't look a day over sixty, and pretty with it!'

'Don't you try and wheedle me, young man,' said Nanny severely, then smiled with pleasure. 'Where have you been?'

'Oh, doing this and that.' He put a parcel on the bed beside her. 'I saw this and somehow it looked like you. Go on, open it.'

There was a gossamer-fine wool stole inside, pink and pretty. He tossed it around the old lady's shoulders and stood back to admire the effect.

'Just right, wouldn't you say, Isobel?' he wanted to know.

'It's charming and suits Mrs Olbinski beautifully. Would you like tea, Dr Winter?'

'Tea? No, thanks, I had something…' He turned to look at her. 'You need some fresh air. I've arranged for the woman who comes here to help in the house to do the same for us. She'll be here in the morning and come again after lunch—you can be free for a couple of hours then. Why not go into the garden now for half an hour? I'll be here.'

Isobel thanked him quietly, got her coat and went down the stairs and into the quiet little garden. It was chilly now but peaceful; there were birds twittering and the sound of traffic, nicely muffled. There was a wooden bench under one of the lilac trees and she sat down, listening to the faint sounds coming from the old houses around her. They were faint because the walls were thick, but presently the windows began to glow with lights and there was a pleasant smell of something delicious cooking. It mingled with the lilacs and she sat sniffing appreciatively. When her half hour was up she went back indoors, hung her coat in the hall, and went straight to the kitchen. There was a light in Nanny's room and the door was half open. There was a light in the sitting room too, but she didn't go in.

The potatoes were on the boil, the onion was chopped and she was making the pastry for her pie when Dr Winter flung open the door.

'There you are,' he declared unnecessarily. 'You weren't in the garden—I imagined you getting lost in Stockholm. Why do you creep in and out so that no one knows where you are?' He sounded so angry that she paused in the rolling of the pastry to stare at him.

'But I've been in the garden,' she told him patiently. 'I came in at the end of half an hour—you said half an hour.' Her voice became very slightly shrill with annoyance. 'Do I have to report on and off duty, then?'

'Good God no! I thought…never mind what I thought. Nanny's asleep again. When you've done that come into the sitting room and have a drink.'

Isobel put her pie in the oven, put the potatoes to cool, found a frying pan and set everything ready for her promised *pommes Lyonnaises*. This done, she went into the sitting room. The doctor was standing with his hands in his pockets, staring out of the window, but he turned to look at her as she sat down. 'I thought you wanted to change your dress,' he observed.

She gave him a pitying look. 'I haven't had a chance,' she pointed out mildly.

'Ah, no, of course not. Stupid of me. Can dinner wait while you do whatever you want to do?'

'Yes, it can, if you don't mind it being half an hour later. And if you wouldn't mind going to Mrs Olbinski if she wants anything…'

He nodded and handed her a glass. 'Well, have your drink before you go.'

There was no reason why he should be eager for her society, even for five minutes. She had long ago accepted the fact that a quiet manner and a plain face held little attraction for a man, especially for Dr Winter, who presumably could pick and choose, bearing in mind the advantages of good looks, a splendid house and, presumably, an equally splendid job in the medical profession. Isobel drank the sherry rather too fast, murmured vaguely and went back to the kitchen where she rearranged her cooking and then went to her room, peeping in on Mrs Olbinski on the way.

She felt better after a shower. She would have liked time to wash her hair but that would have to wait; she brushed it smooth, made up her face in a moderate sort of way, put on the pleated skirt and the Liberty print blouse and went back to the sitting room.

'Supper will be about twenty minutes,' she announced from the door.

The doctor was at the window again, his back to the TV which he had switched on. He looked her up and down. He said: 'Ah, this is to be a special occasion, is it?' in a silky voice she didn't care about—there was, after all, no reason to mock her. She went to the kitchen, shut the door and put on the apron behind it.

The pie was baked. She took it from the oven and the fragrance of it brought the doctor into the kitchen. He eyed it with the same look which her younger brother would have bestowed on it. He said with an endearing boyishness: 'I like pie…I'm hungry.'

'Well, you shall have it, after the chops.' She was assembling the *pommes Lyonnaises* with small competent hands; the smell as she tossed the mixture into the hot oil in the pan caused the doctor to sniff appreciatively.

'I can't think why you haven't been snapped up by some discerning man,' he observed lightly. 'You may be a good nurse, but you appear to be a cook of the first water.'

'A good plain cook,' she reminded him gently, and laid a tray for Mrs Olbinski, not looking at him. He had sat himself on the edge of the table, and was eating a roll. 'That will take the edge off your appetite,' she warned him, and skimmed away to the dining alcove to lay the table. When she got back he had seen to the wine, found the glasses and wandered to the table with them, and since Mrs Olbinski's tray was ready, took it to her room while Isobel sat her up against her pillows.

The old lady inspected the contents of her tray with a sharp eye. 'It looks very nice,' she conceded. 'What's for pudding?'

Isobel told her. 'But if you'd rather, I'll make you a custard…'

'Certainly not!' declared Mrs Olbinski. 'I'm still young enough to enjoy a good fruit pie. Have you a light hand with pastry?'

'So they say,' said Isobel, and went away to dish

up, leaving the doctor to pour a glass of wine for his charge.

She had a glass candle light in the centre of the table and a small nosegay of flowers on either side of it. The alcove glowed in its gentle light. Isobel began to carry in the dishes and Dr Winter, pouring the wine, observed in what she described to herself as his mocking voice: 'In any other circumstances this could be described as a romantic setting.'

'Well, we can soon change that,' said Isobel matter-of-factly, and whisked away the glass candle light from the table and switched on the bright overhead light above the table.

When she came back with the next lot of dishes she heard him say mildly: 'I didn't say I disliked it, Isobel.'

For such a serene girl the look she gave him was quite ferocious. 'No? Anyway, it wasn't my intention. Would you like your salad now or after the chops?'

'Oh, now, I think. I've annoyed you.' He waited until she had sat down and then sat down himself. The brilliant lighting did nothing to detract from his good looks; she wondered crossly what sort of adverse effect it was having upon her own unremarkable features. She said stiffly: 'Not in the least, Dr Winter,' and ate her salad in silence.

He followed her into the kitchen presently and carried in the dishes for her, then said in his mildest voice: 'If you would like to telephone anyone from here, you can do so easily. There's an extension in the hall and I'll get the number for you.'

'Oh, thank you, I'd love to. You—you don't know when we'll be back in England?'

'No, it depends largely on Nanny, but we shall be here for at least two days—I want her really fit. The delay in Gdansk shook her up a bit.'

Isobel passed him the dish of *pommes Lyonnaises* and he took a second helping. 'Did you expect that?' she asked.

'Yes, I hoped it could be avoided, but I wasn't surprised.'

'And not anxious that she wouldn't be allowed to leave?'

'Anxious? My dear girl, I was scared out of my wits!'

'You're joking!'

'No, although I have no intention of admitting that to anyone else. There is something else I must admit to you; you are, after all, most suitable, Isobel.' He got up from the table, fetched the candle light and set it between them and turned off the overhead lamp. 'I'm not being romantic,' he explained, 'merely offering my—well, no, let's say that I'm showing my appreciation.'

A remark she would have to think about later on. Now she collected up the dishes and while he took them into the kitchen, went to see how Mrs Olbinski was getting on. She had eaten everything. 'Very well cooked,' she pronounced. 'I couldn't have done it better myself. Where's that pie?'

The pie was demolished and they washed up before they had their coffee, and by then it was time to settle Mrs Olbinski for the night. When Isobel went back to the sitting room it was to find Dr Winter deep in a book, so she wished him goodnight and went away again. He had got up when she went in, but he had kept his finger in the page as though he couldn't wait to get back to it, impatient to see her gone. I mustn't get so sensitive, she told herself, tumbling into bed. I daresay the book's far more interesting than I am. But he had enjoyed her cooking, on that pleasing thought she slept.

The next morning held no idle moments. There was Nanny to see to, and although the helper came after breakfast, there was lunch to prepare and a load of washing to put into the machine. The doctor took himself off after they had had coffee and he had taken a look at Mrs Olbinski. He would bring back bread and the groceries she needed, he told Isobel, and she watched him go with something like envy. It was a fine day and she longed for a chance to escape for a couple of hours; perhaps this afternoon while Mrs Olbinski had her nap, when it might be possible for her to go out if Helga was in the flat. She did her chores, got lunch, saw Helga off home with the promise that she would return at two o'clock, and sat down to wait for Dr Winter.

She had taken the opportunity of ringing her

mother while he was out, and that lady, although delighted to hear from her, expressed no impatience when she said that she might be back a few days later than she had expected. 'The weather is dreadful here, darling,' said her mother comfortably, 'so stay as long as you can. It sounded a nice case—I hope it is, dear?'

'Yes, oh yes, Mother. I'll tell you all about it when I get back.'

Mrs Olbinski had called then and she had hung up.

They lunched off an omelette, light as thistledown, and rolls and cheese and fruit and another pot of coffee. 'When did Helga say she'd be back?' asked the doctor as he began washing up.

'Two o'clock.'

'Well, go and get Nanny settled and then fetch your jacket, you're due some time off.'

Isobel needed no second bidding. Fifteen minutes or so later she poked her nose round the sitting room door. Helga was there, talking in her peculiar English to Dr Winter. 'What time do you want me back?' asked Isobel.

The doctor nodded to Helga and came to the door. 'We'll be back about five o'clock; Helga knows just what to do and I've told Nanny where we're going.'

'We?'

'You'll see so much more if you're with someone who knows his way around,' said Dr Winter smugly.

'There's really no need...' began Isobel, regretting very much that there wasn't.

'I'm responsible for you while you're in my employ,' said the doctor blandly—a remark destined to banish any half-formed ideas in her head.

All the same the afternoon was a delight. They spent an hour wandering around the old town, and Isobel bought a Dala horse for her mother and a leather belt for her brother, borrowing the money from the doctor, and then, since he said that it was a shame not to get them while she had the chance, she bought some of the lovely coloured candles displayed in all the shops. It seemed logical to buy one or two candle holders to go with them.

'You'll keep a careful account, won't you?' asked Isobel.

'Every single *ore*,' promised Dr Winter.

They took a taxi and drove out to the Millesgarden. An absolute must, he explained; Milles was Sweden's famous modern sculptor and his work wasn't to be missed on any account. And he was right. The garden overlooked the Baltic and had been built in terraces, screened by silver birches and firs and flower beds, and the sculptures, cunningly arranged on the terraces, were each a work of art. Isobel, going slowly, stopping by each one, quite forgot the doctor patiently waiting beside her. Only when they reached the last terrace and she saw The Hand of God, did she put out a hand and clutch his sleeve.

'Oh, look—do look, isn't it marvellous? I've never seen anything like it. It's…there's no way of describing it…'

The doctor looked down at her animated face. It

was astonishing that such a very ordinary face could become almost beautiful once its owner was aroused.

He said placidly: 'It is a marvellous work. Come and look at the fountain, and if you look up there you can see Milles' house and studio. We'll go back that way, but I expect you'd like to go to the last terrace and get a view of the Baltic.'

There were not many people about; it was a little early for tourists, he told her. In another month the roses would be out and it would be a good deal warmer.

'And in winter?' asked Isobel, staring up at Man and Pegasus, her eyes wide and her mouth a little open.

'If the snow's deep it makes sightseeing here rather tricky.'

'Oh, of course. Have you been in Stockholm in the winter?'

'That's when I prefer to come.' He was leading her up the stone steps towards Milles' house and the exit.

'Oh, skiing…'

'Yes.'

'Is it difficult?'

'No, not if you want to do it.' He looked at her small, neat figure. 'You should do well, I think.'

'Well, I don't suppose I'll get the chance to learn,' she observed matter-of-factly. 'I expect you want to get back to the flat.'

He looked amused. 'Do I? But tea first, I think.'

They took a taxi back to the centre of the city and

had tea in a small and elegant tea room; the kind of tea Isobel so seldom had a chance to enjoy—thin china cups with lemon and mountainous cream cakes.

'Feel like a walk?' asked Dr Winter as they went back into the street. And when she nodded, he plunged into a complex of narrow lanes which eventually brought them out within a stone's throw of the flat. He waved aside her thanks as they entered the flat and went to speak to Helga, while Isobel went to her own room and then to Mrs Olbinski.

The old lady looked remarkably frail against her pillows, but she wanted to hear exactly where they had been and what they had done. Supper would have to be late, decided Isobel, embarking on a blow-by-blow account of their afternoon.

As it turned out, that didn't matter. When she eventually left Mrs Olbinski, she found the doctor in the sitting room, looking impatient.

'I shall be out to dinner,' he told her, in a cool remote voice quite at variance with his friendly manner during the afternoon. 'I've got a key, so go to bed and lock the door. I'll go and see Nanny before I go. How does she seem?'

She stifled her disappointment under a calm front. 'Tired, although she's been in bed almost all of today. Should I get her up for an hour or two, just for supper?'

He started for the door. 'I'll let you know. Give her a light meal and see she takes her tablets.'

Isobel went into the kitchen and looked in the cupboards and fridge. She had planned dinner in her mind—smoked salmon vol-au-vents, Swedish meat balls and stuffed cabbage rolls and an egg custard for afters. Now it need only be a light egg dish and probably soup and some fruit to finish with. The doctor came into the kitchen presently, ready to go out again. He had changed his clothes, she noticed, and had another shave. He gave a careless glance round the kitchen. 'Nanny's all right; not as spry as I could wish, but her pulse is stronger. If she's no worse tomorrow I'll get seats on a plane for the day after. Get her up by all means. If you want me urgently get this number.' He scribbled on the kitchen pad. 'Goodnight, Isobel.'

She wished him goodnight in a bright voice and busied herself at once getting out bowls and eggs, butter and a can of soup. Only when she heard the door close did she put everything down and go along to Mrs Olbinski. For some reason she didn't want to be alone with her thoughts.

The evening seemed very long. Mrs Olbinski didn't want to get up for her supper; Isobel washed her and made her bed, turned on the TV for her and went to make an omelette and a warm drink. It wasn't until much later, when the old lady had dozed off, that she went back into the kitchen to get her own meal. To cook for one was absurd, so she boiled an egg, found a roll and butter and sat at the kitchen table with a magazine, and then because the TV was still in Mrs Olbinski's room and she didn't want to disturb her, she took herself off to bed. She stayed awake for a long time, but Dr Winter hadn't returned by the time she went to sleep.

Rather to her surprise, he offered to take her sightseeing again the next morning, but as she pointed out, even with Helga there, she had the ironing to do and Mrs Olbinski to care for.

He didn't appear to mind whether she accepted or not, merely told her to take an hour off after lunch. 'I'll go along and get seats on an afternoon flight for tomorrow,' he told her. 'Nanny is no worse—no better either, but I think we'd better get her home. Helga will be here at two o'clock and you can safely leave her then.'

Isobel spent a busy morning, what with her patient, who was rather fretful, the ironing, and the preparation of the evening meal. By the time the doctor came back she had rolls and butter, cheese and cold meat on the table and a mouthwatering salad.

The doctor was politely friendly as they ate, helped her clear the dishes ready for Helga to wash presently and then went along to talk to Mrs Olbinski. He didn't stay long; Isobel made the old lady comfortable for her nap, promised she would be back within the hour, and fetched her jacket. Helga was already in the kitchen and the doctor was in the sitting room, but she reached the little hall and he joined her, opened the door and went down the stairs with her. Just for a few moments she thought that he intended accompanying her on her walk, but as they reached the archway to the road he said casually: 'Well, have a pleasant hour, Isobel,' and turned away in the direction of Storkyrkan. She had intended to pay the church another visit, but now she went briskly in the other direction, hoping she looked as though she knew where she was going. She was quickly lost, of course, but there were always the tall church spires to guide her. She pottered through the charming cobbled streets, peering in the windows of the small expensive antique shops, jewellers and boutiques, but after half an hour she made her way back to the great church and spent the remainder of her free time there, wandering up and down its splendid wide aisles and standing to stare at the fifteenth-century statue of St George and the Dragon. She stayed so long that she had to hurry back to the flat and got there just in time to answer Mrs Olbinski's fretful voice demanding tea.

She had a cup with the old lady and stayed to chat with her for a little while, and then because she was still fretful, wrapped her in her pink stole and helped her to the kitchen. She settled her there in a well cushioned chair, wrapped a blanket round her knees, and started to get things ready for their evening meal. Dr Winter found them there presently, Isobel busy with the vol-au-vents and Mrs Olbinski with a bowl and an egg whisk, preparing the eggs for the custard.

Mrs Olbinski stayed up for dinner, sitting between them in the dining alcove, her peevishness forgotten, telling them tales of her life in Poland, and when the doctor suggested at last that she should go to bed, she went happily enough and fell asleep at once, like a small child.

The doctor had almost finished the washing up by the time Isobel got back to the kitchen. She made more coffee and carried it through to the sitting room, where she listened quietly to his plans for the next day and since he showed no desire for conversation, she wished him goodnight and went to bed. There was, after all, she told herself reasonably, no earthly reason why he should want her company; she was there to look after Mrs Olbinski and he had no interest in her beyond the fact that she was a nurse, there to do a job for him. She speculated if things might have been different—if she had been blue-eyed and pretty and a clever talker—and studying her commonplace reflection in the dressing table glass thought that it was very likely they would. She nodded to herself as she brushed her hair. 'This time next week, he'll have forgotten you.' She said it very firmly.

The flight left at two o'clock from Arlanda Airport, thirty-eight kilometres from the city. Isobel spent a busy morning getting Mrs Olbinski up and dressed, preparing an early lunch for them all, packing their few things and helping Helga to tidy the flat. A taxi took them there, and since there was time to spare, Isobel and Mrs Olbinski were settled in the bar, given coffee and a handful of papers and magazines while the doctor went off to see about their luggage. He didn't come back until their flight was called, and this time he had a wheelchair with him. Mrs Olbinski, half asleep, made no objection to being put into it, and once at the plane, he carried her up the steps, settled her in a window seat, told Isobel to sit beside her and settled himself on the other side of the aisle. He must be relieved to have the business finished, thought Isobel, watching him unfold *The Times*. He had become aloof since they had left the flat, as though he was looking forward to seeing the last of her, and he had answered her vaguely when she had asked if he required her services once they got to his house. There would be servants enough to help Mrs Olbinski; she began to speculate on how to get herself home as quickly as possible.

Of course he might dismiss her at Heathrow, but that was unlikely; she felt sure he would at least ascertain that she could get home as easily as possible. If she could telephone her mother before she left his house and catch a bus…he might even allow her the taxi fare. She would go along to the agency in the morning in the hope that he had paid promptly, and see about another case, that would give her the rest of the day to see to her clothes and tell her mother all her news. She would have gone on for some time making plans, only Mrs Olbinski, who had dropped off again, awoke and wanted tea, and while she had it, wanted to know how soon it would be before they were home. 'Because I'm tired,' she said in a rather thin voice. 'Everything's happened so quickly and I shall feel so strange…I'm so glad you'll be there, Isobel.'

It seemed hardly the time to say that that wasn't
very likely. Isobel edged the conversation round to
the old lady's memories of life in Poland, and hoped
that the awkward moment was over.

It seemed as though it was. They landed presently,
and throughout the business of getting themselves out
of the plane, in and out of Customs, finding a porter,
and collecting luggage, scarcely a word was spoken.
The doctor, as usual, had everything in hand. There
was no hitch, and they were outside on the pavement
in no time at all and before Isobel had time to wonder
what happened next, a dark blue Rolls-Royce crept to
a halt beside them. The driver got out, exchanged a
few words with Dr Winter, helped the porter stow the
luggage and disappeared. The doctor lifted Mrs Olbinski into the back seat, nodded to Isobel to get in
beside her and took the wheel. He hadn't spoken except to ask if Nanny was comfortable and it was difficult to shout questions at his back. Isobel settled
back in luxury. When they reached his house she
would find out exactly what he expected of her, and
at the same time point out, in the most reasonable
manner possible, that he might have had the good
manners to keep her informed beforehand. He was a
tiresome man, she mused silently, far too sure of himself. She paused—well, being sure of himself had
helped in Poland, she supposed, and once or twice he
had been quite friendly. It was a waste of time thinking about him anyway, so she turned her attention to
Mrs Olbinski who, now that they were approaching
London, was getting excited.

CHAPTER FOUR

DR WINTER'S HOUSEHOLD apparently ran on oiled wheels. The glossy front door was opened as the car drew up before it and the same impassive manservant came down the steps, greeted Dr Winter with a warmth which lightened his solemn features to a surprising extent, and opened the door for her to get out. Isobel found herself going into the house behind the doctor with Mrs Olbinski in his arms and, once there, following him through a massive mahogany door into a long room with windows at both ends; it was an elegant room; she hoped that she would have time to look round it properly before she went, but just for the moment her patient was her main concern. The terrible hat had to be lifted from a tired elderly head, the shabby coat carefully removed and their owner settled in a comfortable chair.

'I'd like a cup of tea,' declared Nanny in a thready voice, and the doctor nodded to a stout cosy woman who had hurried to meet them as they entered the room. 'For all of us,' he added.

But when it came, he refused his, went to a sofa table against one of the walls and poured himself a whisky, before sitting down in a wingback chair by the empty fireplace. He raised his glass to the old lady. 'Welcome home, Nanny,' he said. 'Tomorrow we'll celebrate together, but it's been a long day; how about early bed and a nice supper on a tray?' He glanced at Isobel. 'Ah, yes—and you, Isobel…'

He was interrupted by the door being flung open and a light laughing voice exclaiming, 'It's all right, Gibson, I know my way,' and a girl came in—tall, slim, dramatically dark, wearing clothes Isobel had studied in the glossy magazines with a strong envy.

She ran across the room on preposterous heels and flung herself at Dr Winter. 'Thomas—why didn't you let me know you would be back? There's this party this evening and I've been so miserable thinking you wouldn't be here to take me—now you can.' She flung her arms round his neck and kissed him. 'Where've you been?'

She unwound herself and glanced at Nanny and Isobel sitting side by side, each very upright in her chair. 'Who ever are these people?'

He took her arm. 'Come and meet my old nanny, Mrs Olbinski, who's coming to live with me, and this is Miss Barrington, a nurse who's been looking after her. He smiled at Nanny. 'This is Miss Ella Stokes, Nanny—Isobel.'

Miss Stokes smiled tepidly at Nanny and coldly at Isobel. 'The party is at half past eight—we can eat afterwards, though.'

'I'm afraid not, Ella. We've just this minute got back. You'll have to find someone else. That should be easy enough.'

'Of course it's easy,' said Miss Stokes pettishly, 'but I want you, Thomas.'

'I'm flattered but adamant, darling. I'll give you lunch tomorrow instead.' He sounded amused, but he also sounded as though he meant what he said.

'Oh, all right, but I simply must talk to you—just for a few minutes, please, Thomas?'

'How could I refuse that?' he asked, laughing. 'But wait a minute while I get Nanny upstairs.' He picked up the old lady, looked at Isobel and said: 'Nurse— if you will come too?' and led the way out of the room.

Nanny's room was on the first floor, large, airy and convenient. 'You'll find all you want,' Dr Winter said, setting her down on a chair near the bed. 'If you need anything, ring the bell and Mrs Gibson will come.' He bent to kiss the old lady. 'I'll look in later,' he promised her, and had reached the door by the time Isobel had caught up with him.

'Dr Winter,' her tone was quite decidedly fierce, 'I should like to know...'

He stopped to look at her. 'Ah—of course, Isobel, you want to know where your room is. Mrs Gibson will show you.'

'I didn't know that I was staying for the night here. And do you want to see me before I go in the morning?'

He was staring at her now with a kind of impatient amusement. 'Go? But am I not still employing you? I wasn't aware that I'd mentioned you leaving.'

'No, nor have you, but when you interviewed me you said that you would require my services only until such time as you had a suitable companion for Mrs

Olbinski. Well, you have. Mrs Gibson and she are old friends.'

He said coolly: 'Mrs Gibson is also my house-keeper.'

'That's as may be. I may be only in your temporary employ, Dr Winter, but I merit some of your consid-eration—I've been wholly in the dark…'

'Oh dear, oh dear!' His cool eyes were sparkling with amusement now. 'I see that I must beg pardon. If I ask you nicely will you be kind enough to stay the night, and in the morning we must have a talk. You have another case waiting, perhaps?'

It was a temptation to say yes, but Isobel shook her head.

'In that case…' he smiled at her with sudden charm, 'we'll see each other tomorrow.'

He had gone, along the gallery and then down the staircase, and she heard him answering Ella's laugh-ing voice. Which was no reason why she should feel so forlorn.

But she shook the feeling off as Mrs Gibson came trotting along to join her. 'I've put you in the room next to Nanny's, Nurse dear. There's a bathroom be-tween you, but if you keep the doors open you'll be able to hear if she wants anything.' She bustled ahead and opened a door, ushering Isobel into a charming room, all pale colours and pretty light shades and a carpet to lose one's feet in. 'What an adventure!' went on Mrs Gibson, bent on a nice chat. 'We was all worried when Mr Thomas went off like he did, all secret like, as you might say, though we're that

pleased to have Nanny back with us—twenty years
she's bin gone, but it don't seem that long. Were you
frightened, Nurse?'

Isobel reflected. 'Not frightened, though it was a
little alarming when we were told that Nanny couldn't
leave at once. But Dr Winter knew just what to do.'

She had taken off her jacket and was tidying herself
before the triple mirror on the delicate rosewood table
between the windows.

'You can be sure of that,' agreed Mrs Gibson happily, 'always knows what to do, does our Mr
Thomas.'

Isobel agreed silently, adding the rider that it would
be nice if he would share his plans with others from
time to time. Like that time he disappeared for the
night at Gdansk—just suppose she had wanted him
during the night, or she'd fallen down and broken a
leg…the possibilities of disaster were endless. She
spent quite a few minutes exploring them, rather for-
getful of Mrs Gibson, standing near, watching her.

'Well, if you've got all you want, Nurse, I'll pop
along and see if the doctor wants his dinner at
home—that Miss Stokes is always fussing him to take
her somewhere or other—he needs a quiet evening at
home, if you ask me. There'll be dinner in half an
hour, Nurse. You'll want to get Nanny into her bed
first. When you're ready, just ring the bell and someone will be up with her supper, and I'll come along
and have a chat with her so you can have your dinner
in peace.'

Isobel had Mrs Olbinski comfortably settled in bed

within twenty minutes with a supper tray on the bed table before her, which left her ten minutes in which to get ready for her own meal. It seemed unlikely that the doctor would be joining her; all the same, she changed her blouse, made up her face and did her hair and then went, rather nervously, downstairs.

Gibson was hovering in the hall and his impassive face was very smiling. He opened a door and ushered her into a small room—well, compared to the room she had already been in—it seemed small, it was cosily furnished with glazed chintz covers on the easy chairs and two sofas, one on each side of the fireplace, and the colours were nicely muted. She hadn't expected the doctor to be there, and when he turned round to look at her she said in a surprised voice: 'Oh, you are here!'

'Where else should I be?' he wanted to know. 'This is my home.'

She felt her face glow under his amused look. 'Well, yes, I know that!' she told him patiently, 'but I thought you'd be out with—with Miss Stokes.' And since he went on looking at her and didn't utter a word: 'The party, you know...'

'I seem to remember telling her I wouldn't be going...'

'Oh, I know that, I heard you, but I didn't think you meant it.' Isobel added by way of explanation: 'She's so very pretty.'

'If you knew me better, Isobel, you would know that if I say something I mean it.'

'Always?'

'Always. Would you care for a glass of sherry before we have dinner?'

'Well—thank you, yes. But I don't think I should stay away too long—Mrs Olbinski...'

He interrupted her: 'Mrs Gibson is with her, and they'll have a nice cosy gossip about the old days. It would be most unkind of you to disturb them.'

So Isobel drank her sherry and then crossed the hall with him to the dining room, where amidst its subdued splendour and under the watchful eye of Gibson she ate her dinner; artichoke soup, sole Véronique, *steak au poivre* and a delicious trifle for dessert. She was hungry and ate with a good appetite, drinking the wine poured into her glass and making polite conversation with the doctor. She longed to ask him if she was to leave in the morning, although she was sure she would be going. Mrs Olbinski didn't need a nurse any more and there seemed enough staff in the house to attend to her small wants. As they got up from the table she said: 'I should like to phone my mother, if you don't mind.'

'Of course. There's a telephone in the sitting room across the hall and you won't be disturbed. It will, of course, be useless for you to give any details of your departure from here until we've had our little talk tomorrow, but I'm sure you want to let your mother know you're back in London.'

He opened the door for her and ushered her inside, then left her with a quiet goodnight.

Her mother, although delighted to hear from her, didn't seem to mind that she might not be home for a day or two. 'Although I'm pretty sure I'll be leaving some time tomorrow,' said Isobel, 'only Dr Winter's being pigheaded about telling me.'

'Ah, yes—you did tell me that he wasn't keen on engaging you in the first place. Has he been tiresome?'

Isobel thought about that. 'Well, no, not really. Look, love, I'll give you a ring tomorrow morning and let you know what time I'll get home.'

She was so certain in her own mind that she would be leaving once she had seen the doctor that she had packed her case when she got up on the next morning, although she didn't say anything to Mrs Olbinski when she went along to her room to help her dress and see that she ate her breakfast. And it was almost lunchtime, and she was fuming at the delay, before Mrs Gibson came sailing upstairs to say that the doctor was home and would she be good enough to join him in the study.

His 'good morning' was casual and his apology perfunctory but she was prepared to forgive all that until he added carelessly: 'I should have come straight here, I know, but Ella wanted to see me.'

Isobel said she quite understood, in such a frosty voice that he looked at her sharply, then proceeded to leave her speechless with: 'I phoned the agency this morning—I've engaged you for another week.'

Isobel found her breath again. 'I expected to leave today—this morning,' she told him in a voice, which, despite her anger, came out very calmly. 'You are, if

I may say so, Dr Winter, a very inconsiderate employer.'

He looked interested. 'Am I? I can't think why. After all, nursing is your job, surely it doesn't matter overmuch who or where you nurse? I'd better pay you, hadn't I? The agency reminded me…and you have to have a free day—two, I believe, but perhaps you could manage with one?'

'It seems I have very little choice, but I really must have time to go home and get some more clothes.'

He looked surprised. 'Oh, must you? The ones you're wearing seem quite adequate. But you know best. You can go now if you like—well, after lunch, and be back here for lunch tomorrow. I shall be out, and I'd be happier about Nanny if you are here.'

He sat down at his desk and opened his cheque book, barely glancing at her as he said: 'Do sit down, Isobel.'

She wanted to argue with him, but she couldn't find the right words. She sat rather primly and looked around her. The room was of a pleasant size, its walls lined with bookshelves, the chairs leather-covered and large. There was a table under the window with a chair pulled up to it, its surface scattered with books and papers, and another small table with a reading lamp kept company with an easy chair in a corner. The desk took up a good deal of one wall; it was piled high with papers, books and pamphlets. Isobel longed to tidy it up and wondered what would happen if she did—the doctor would probably go spare. She

pictured Mrs Gibson tiptoeing round with a feather
duster, not disturbing a single sheet of paper.

She glanced at the doctor and found him staring at
her. She went a guilty red and he said: 'You should
learn to hide your thoughts, Isobel; you long to or-
ganise my desk, don't you?' and when she nodded:
'Well, you're not going to.' He got up and came and
stood in front of her so that she had to tilt her head
back to see his face. 'Here's a cheque for your first
week—I'm told that the correct thing is for me to pay
them, but if I did so I daresay you might have to wait
a couple of weeks for your fee, which seems hardly
fair. Don't, whatever you do, give them any of that
money, I'll settle with them separately. How is
Nanny?' he added.

'Very comfortable. She's up and dressed and Mrs
Gibson is with her while I'm here.'

He nodded. 'I'll get her downstairs into the small
sitting room so that anyone passing through the hall
can keep an eye on her. Do you suppose she'd be up
to getting some clothes in a couple of days? When
you get back tomorrow, perhaps? Gibson can drive
you and get her in and out of the shops.' He studied
his nails thoughtfully. 'She'd better go somewhere
they'll have all she needs, then she can sit quietly and
choose everything from her chair.' He wandered off
across the room to look out of the window. 'Better
still, how about you getting a selection of things for
her to choose from? Pretty dresses and so forth.' He
sounded vague and Isobel smiled a little. He turned
round to look at her. 'She's unlikely to go out in the

foreseeable future, but get her a coat and a hat just the same.'

He didn't explain further, but she didn't need to be told, she said quietly: 'Very well, I'll get her measurements and shop when I get back tomorrow.'

'You'd better go to Harrods—I've got an account there. I'll give them a ring presently. Go to the Accounts Department and say who you are. Now shall we have lunch? I've got a busy afternoon before me.'

Just as though she had been hindering him! Isobel thought indignantly.

She got home much sooner than she expected. They had eaten lunch with a minimum of talk, and that concerning Nanny, and after making sure that her patient had all she needed and that Mrs Gibson knew what to do in an emergency, Isobel hurried out of the house. Gibson was standing on the steps and there was a Daimler Sovereign parked at the kerb. He said, 'Good afternoon, Nurse,' just as though he hadn't been serving her lunch not an hour since, took her case from her and opened the car door. 'Dr Winter asked me to drive you to your home. Where would that be, Nurse?'

'Clapham Common—the far side, twenty-four, Jordan Street, and thank you, Gibson.'

'A pleasure, Nurse. I'll fetch you tomorrow at noon, if that suits you?'

A mere figure of speech, of course. Dr Winter would have said noon and noon it would be, whether it suited her or not. 'That would do very well,' she said pleasantly; after all, she shouldn't look a gift horse in the mouth.

Her mother was coming out of the house as Gibson stopped before its door, but she put the key straight back in the lock and opened the door again. 'Darling, how lovely!' She came down the path and smiled at Gibson and when Isobel introduced him offered a hand. 'You have no idea what an awkward journey it is from your part of the world to ours,' she commented chattily. 'Can I offer you tea before you go back?'

Gibson's boot face had become quite human. 'Thank you, no, ma'am, I have to get back at once. I'll be here at noon tomorrow to drive you back, Nurse.'

He got out of the car and carried Isobel's case to the door, wished them good day and drove off.

'Goodness me,' observed Mrs Barrington, 'he's like something out of another world—I mean, you just don't meet people like that any more; they wear jeans and long hair and call you love.'

'Dr Winter has got a house full of people just like Gibson,' said Isobel, and hugged her mother. 'I'm to stay there another week, and I've got my first week's cheque—I'm supposed to wait and get it from the agency, but Dr Winter bends rules when they don't suit him.' She picked up her case. 'I'll dump this lot in my room and we'll do the shopping. I've got twenty-four hours off to get some more clothes, and I must get my uniforms washed ready for the next case...'

'That will give me something to do when you've gone again, darling. I haven't much shopping, let's get it done and then have an early tea and a good gossip. I'm longing to hear about your trip and the old lady...' Mrs Barrington was longing to hear about Dr Winter too, but she was too cunning to say so. A few questions carefully put, later on...

She didn't glean much, though. Isobel, accustomed to telling her mother almost everything concerning her own doings, found herself quite unable to talk about the doctor. She admitted that he was good-looking, quite young, presumably comfortably off, devoted to his old nanny and living in some style, but these sparse titbits were all that Mrs Barrington was offered. She was left frustrated and intrigued; Isobel was being remarkably reticent. She reflected that Isobel would be there for another week—a lot could happen in a week. Mrs Barrington's daydreams might be farfetched and absurd, but she was a devoted mother; Isobel would make a specially splendid wife and Dr Winter was unmarried, surely their rather unusual journey to Gdansk had provided just the right background for romance?

Luckily for her she wasn't there when Isobel met Dr Winter on her return the next day. He was coming down the stairs as she entered the house and growled out a greeting from a face as black as thunder. Isobel wasn't to know that Nanny had been reading him a lecture, blandly ignoring the fact that he was a grown man and not the small boy she had looked after so lovingly. It was time that he married, she had told him in no uncertain terms—'And not that pert miss who came upstairs unasked to see me while she was waiting for you to come home yesterday afternoon,' Nanny breathed fire. 'She called me Nanny, the saucebox!'

The doctor had preserved a calm manner, but he had had a tiring busy morning at the hospital and it was years since anyone had even made a timid attempt to query his lifestyle or what he did and why. He had cut the old lady politely short and with the excuse that he had work to do, had made for his study, only to meet Isobel's placid gaze as he reached the bottom of the staircase. The calm enquiry in her look incensed him even more and he snapped: 'You're late!'

Isobel might be unassuming in appearance, but a loud cross voice and beetle brows left her unmoved. 'No, I'm not,' she spoke in the soothing voice she would have used towards a difficult patient or a grumpy child. 'You said noon, Dr Winter.'

There was a magnificent grandfather clock at the foot of the stairs. It wheezed obligingly and began a ponderous striking; it took some time to get to the last of the twelve chimes. 'You see?' observed Isobel kindly. 'I daresay you've had a busy morning.'

'My God,' said Dr Winter, 'you're as bad as Nanny!' He disappeared into his study and shut the door with a restrained slam. Isobel went on up the stairs to her room and then along to see how Mrs Olbinski fared.

The old lady was glad to see her. 'I've been a bit

lonely, as you might say,' she observed, 'not but what it's a pleasure to have old friends round me but you've got a way with you, I suppose. I'll have my lunch now you're back and I've made a list of the clothes Mr Thomas says I'm to have, only you'll need to measure me.' She looked sideways at Isobel. 'In a temper, he is, just because I told him not to marry that silly young woman…' A slow tear trickled down one cheek, and Isobel wiped it away gently and put an arm round the thin shoulders.

'I wondered why he was cross when I came in,' she remarked matter-of-factly. 'But I'm sure he'll have forgotten all about it in no time at all. Look, how about measuring you before lunch, then I'll go down and see what there is for you. Do you fancy anything special?'

'A nice little lamb chop with a bit of mashed potato and one of Mrs Gibson's jelly creams. It's not like him to be angry. Perhaps I shouldn't have come here…I'm going to be a nuisance to him.' Another tear had to be wiped away.

'Now that's nonsense and you know it, Mrs Olbinski.' Isobel dropped a kiss on her patient's cheek and busied herself with notebook and pen and the tape measure Mrs Olbinski had in her handbag, and presently in the excitement of being measured for new clothes and weighing the advantages of navy blue against brown, Mrs Olbinski cheered up.

Lunch was at one o'clock. Isobel saw her patient comfortably settled at a small table with her lunch before her and went downstairs to the dining room.

She felt sure she would be on her own. Dr Winter was in no mood for company, but he was there, standing in front of his fireplace with his hands in his pockets and an expressionless face. Still cross, she decided, and took her place wordlessly.

There was no conversation with the soup. He was behaving like a small spoilt boy, and she found it surprisingly pathetic. She said cheerfully: 'My mother was very glad to see me; it was kind of you to send me home in the car and fetch me back as well.'

'I'm delighted to hear it.' He waved away the pudding Gibson was offering. 'You'll excuse me, I have a busy afternoon ahead of me. Take a taxi to Harrods and return in one, Isobel.'

She said cheerfully: 'Oh, but the walk will do me good…'

'Be so good as to do as I ask. You'll be reimbursed.'

She started indignantly: 'Well, I had no intention…' but he had gone.

Even if she had wanted to, she had no chance to disobey him. Gibson had a taxi waiting for her when she came downstairs to leave the house, and to tell the truth, she was glad to have one back, she had so many boxes and parcels. The amount of money she had spent made her feel quite faint, although she was well within the limit Dr Winter had set—indeed, the saleslady, knowing this, had tried hard to sell her a fur-lined raincoat, assuring her that it would be a most useful garment for an elderly lady.

'She's not very active,' observed Isobel, and eyed

the garment with envy. Dr Winter's bride would be a lucky young woman; if he didn't cavil at a few hundred pounds for his old nanny, he certainly wouldn't begrudge his wife a magnificent wardrobe.

She was back at the house by five o'clock, which just went to show, she reflected, that if one had sufficient money, one could buy all one wanted in a couple of hours if necessary.

Gibson, ever on the alert, fetched in her parcels from the taxi and carried them upstairs. 'I don't suppose you had time for tea, Nurse?' he asked.

'Well, no, Gibson, I didn't, but it's rather late...'

'Not at all, Nurse, it shall be brought up to Nanny's room.'

She gave him a grateful smile. 'That's very kind of you, Gibson. I'm sorry to give you the trouble.'

'If I may say so, Nurse, you're no trouble to myself or anyone else working here.'

Isobel flung off her jacket and hurried to Nanny's room, to find that lady in a ferment of excitement. They spent the next hour or more unwrapping things and trying them on. 'You said navy blue or brown,' said Isobel, 'but when I saw this dress I knew it would suit you.' She held up a fine wool dress in a paisley pattern of soft blues and deep red. 'Isn't it pretty? And these slippers—so soft, and don't you love the little bows on them? You'll have to get up every day, Mrs Olbinski, so you can wear all these pretty things.' She rummaged among the piles of tissue paper. 'And I bought this hat, although they said if you didn't like it I could return it. It matches the coat very well.' She popped a smart matronly velvet toque on her patient's head and handed her a mirror. 'Isn't it smashing?'

'Oh, decidedly,' said Dr Winter from the door. 'We'll have to take you out in that, Nanny, it deserves a larger audience than two.' He came into the room and bent to kiss her cheek. 'Has Isobel chosen well? Is there anything you still need?'

The old lady caught his hand and held it tightly. 'Mr Thomas, you've given me everything I've ever wanted—all these lovely clothes and living in your beautiful house and having this dear child to look after me.'

'You looked after me for a good many years, Nanny,' he reminded her cheerfully. 'Would you like to come down to dinner this evening? It's a chance to wear that new dress.'

So Isobel dressed Mrs Olbinski up in the new dress, put on the pretty slippers, arranged her hair nicely and led her to the wall mirror to have a look.

'Well, I never—I am smart, aren't I?' declared Nanny. She turned to Isobel. 'A lot of trouble it must have been for you, child.' She paused. 'You can call me Nanny.'

'Oh, may I? You wouldn't think it too familiar? I mean, I hardly know you or anyone here, and I'll be gone in a few days, you know.'

Nanny gave her a sharp look. 'Yes, well, I suppose there's those that might need you more than I do. I'll be sorry to see you go, though. And not only me will be sorry. Now sit me down somewhere, dear, and go and pretty yourself up.'

Isobel spent five precious minutes deciding whether to wear the Marks and Spencer cotton voile new for the summer or a cream linen dress of impeccable taste which did nothing for her except to make her look older than she was and douse her mousey hair to even greater mousiness. She decided on the linen; it seemed suitable for her status in the household and no one was likely to give her a second glance.

She was mistaken there. The doctor looked at her several times, wondering why she had made no attempt to make the most of her not unattractive person. She looked like a strict governess or a frightfully efficient personal assistant to some executive; all she needed was a pair of specs. She looked up once and caught him staring at her and put up a questing hand to tidy her hair, looking faintly questioning, and because he was essentially a kind man he said: 'You look very nice, Isobel,' and watched her pinken with pleasure. Poor girl, he mused, sipping his whisky, she's had to put up with quite a lot during the last week. He laid himself out to be pleasant, making Nanny laugh and Isobel smile widely, and felt relief when Gibson appeared in the doorway to say that dinner was served.

There was a commotion in the hall as he spoke and Ella Stokes darted past him to fling herself at the doctor.

'Thomas, you beast!' she shrilled. 'You wouldn't take me out this evening, so I've come to see for myself what's stopping you.' She glanced at Mrs Olbinski and Isobel and dismissed them; there was nothing about either of them, in her opinion, to prevent him leaving them alone for the evening. She put up a hand and straightened his tie and he frowned a little. 'Look, I dressed up specially for you,' she wheedled. 'It's new—do you like it?'

She twirled round, and expensive chiffon and silk floated beguilingly round her. 'We'll have to go somewhere quiet because you haven't changed, but there's a little Italian place...'

Dr Winter took her hand very gently from his tie. 'Sorry, Ella, we're having a little celebration dinner in honour of Nanny.'

She pouted prettily. 'Oh, Nanny wouldn't mind— would you, Nanny?' she asked over her shoulder, to be met by one of Nanny's glacial stares, perfected after years of dealing with naughty children. Ella wilted a little but recovered enough to add: 'You've got Nurse—it is Nurse, isn't it?—to keep you company.'

'But I mind, Ella,' said the doctor quietly, 'and I'm having my dinner here in my own house because I want to.'

Ella's pretty face was ugly with rage for a moment, but the next instant her smile was as sweet as ever. 'OK, darling Thomas, so you'd better invite me to join you. I'm not going home to eat something on a tray in a brand new dress that's cost the earth.'

It was impossible to tell if Dr Winter was pleased or not. Isobel, sitting quietly on the fringe of things, couldn't even begin to guess. She finished her drink and watched Ella skilfully take over the conversation.

She could be very amusing, and whether the doctor was pleased that she was there or not, she had him laughing long before Gibson came for the second time to say that dinner was served.

She was the life and soul of the evening after that, praising the food, toasting Nanny, who stared back at her with eyes like pebbles, ignoring Isobel completely except to remark unforgivably: 'You shouldn't wear that colour, you know—it makes you a complete non-person, no colour—you haven't much anyway, have you? I suppose being in that dreary uniform stunts any dress sense you might have.'

Isobel said nothing, although her head teemed with rude words. It was Dr Winter who answered for her. 'You're quite wrong, Ella,' he declared. 'I thought how nice Isobel looked. I should imagine that her taste is excellent.'

'There are some,' began Nanny weightily, 'who have no taste in clothes but enough money to go to a shop where they'll be fitted out right. And we don't all need to dress like peacocks and flaunt our bosoms to catch a man's eye.'

Isobel, who had been feeling like crying, found herself stifling a giggle but a glance at the doctor's face told her that for once she was seeing him out of his depth. She said in her calm way: 'Clothes are a fascinating topic, aren't they? and some of them are so lovely—I could have spent a fortune in Harrods...'

Ella turned her blue eyes on her. 'Harrods? Isn't Marks and Spencer more in your line?'

'Oh, yes,' said Isobel, still calm, 'I was getting

some things for Mrs Olbinski. We couldn't bring back
much with us, you see.'

'Oh, that boring trip!' declared Ella. She turned a
ravishing smile on Dr Winter. 'You're really rather a
darling, rescuing people from dreary places.'

'I wouldn't call Poland dreary even under present
conditions, as a matter of fact, we had a couple of
very pleasant days there, didn't we, Nanny?'

He went on from there talking about this and that,
keeping away from personal matters, but for Mrs Olbinski the evening was spoilt, and for Isobel too, although she told herself that it didn't matter in the least
what the wretched girl said. She would probably
never see her again, only it would be a great pity if
Ella married Dr Winter. She was a clever young
woman, used to getting her own way. Nanny would
be out of the house and into some old people's home
before the doctor would know what was happening.

It was a good thing that shortly after dinner Mrs
Olbinski declared that she was tired and wanted to go
to bed, so that Isobel naturally enough went with her,
wishing Ella goodnight as she went upstairs behind
the doctor carrying Nanny. Before he left them he
invited Isobel to join them again once Nanny was
settled. Her refusal was pleasant and firm; the less she
saw of the horrid creature downstairs the better.

Nanny wasn't all that tired; she had a great deal to
say about ill-bred young women who should know
better. 'The impertinence of her!' she fumed in her
peevish old voice. 'Inviting herself to dinner for all
the world as though she was one of the family! What

Mr Thomas sees in her I do not know.' Her voice came muffled by the nightgown Isobel was drawing over her head. 'And don't you listen to a word she says, Isobel—you look like a lady in that dress, and very nice you were when she was so rude. You might have come from my nursery.' Which remark Isobel recognised as the greatest compliment.

'I had a nanny when I was small,' she told her companion. 'She left to get married when I went to school; she lives in Australia and she still writes to me.'

Mrs Olbinski nodded. 'You're a lady, that I can see—knew it the moment I clapped eyes on you. Fallen on hard times, have you?'

Isobel tucked her into her bed and then sat down on its edge.

'Well, yes. My father died ten years ago and we had to leave my home. We live at Clapham Common, a little terraced house, and my mother is quite wonderful about it. I've got a brother too—he's at school and very clever. He'll go on to university...'

'And that's why you're a nurse.' Nanny patted her hand gently. 'Wouldn't you rather be in a hospital?'

'Yes, of course, but private nursing is well paid, you see.' She added cheerfully, 'It's interesting too, I never know what sort of case I shall get next.' She bent and kissed an elderly cheek. 'Now you're going to sleep. I'm going to bed too. Goodnight, Nanny.'

She was eating a solitary breakfast the next morning when Dr Winter came into the dining room. He didn't bother with a 'good morning'. 'I'm sorry about yesterday evening; Ella doesn't mean half the things she says—she's an only child, and spoilt...'

'Please don't apologise, Dr Winter. It didn't matter a bit, although I think Nanny was a bit upset, that's because she's got a bit out of touch during the last few years—I mean, people don't behave as they did ten years ago.'

'Perhaps not. Can you suggest anything to make her feel better about it?'

'It would be nice if she could go for a quiet drive now and again—if you could spare Gibson to drive. She's longing to wear her new clothes. She told me that she had a niece living at Peckham Rye.'

'A splendid idea. Of course she can go whenever she wants—we'll manage without Gibson for an hour or two.'

Isobel looked down at her plate. 'I can drive,' she told him quite quietly.

He pulled out a chair and sat down and poured himself some coffee.

'Another of your accomplishments, Isobel? Could you tackle the traffic in town?'

'Yes, I think so.' She wasn't going to tell him that she had often driven her mother up to London after her father had died. She hadn't driven much since, of course, but she wasn't nervous.

'Good, you can have the Sovereign tomorrow afternoon.'

She thanked him quietly, pleasantly surprised that he hadn't heaped her with warnings and doubts as to whether she was capable of driving or not. At least he trusted her; a nice warm glow crept under her ribs and she smiled at nothing in particular. Just for a moment she looked pretty, and the doctor, getting up to go, paused to take another look. She wasn't to be compared with Ella or any of the other young women she supposed he knew, but she was a great deal more restful.

CHAPTER FIVE

THE NEXT FEW DAYS were rather fun. Isobel settled Nanny, dressed in her finery, in the back of the car, got into the driver's seat and once she had gained Vauxhall Bridge, tooled it down the Camberwell Road to Peckham. Of course once she left the main road, she got lost amongst the narrow rows of small brick houses, all exactly alike, but finally she arrived and rang the bell of a similar house, its tiny front garden filled with gnomes and small shrubs struggling to survive. There had been no time to let Nanny's niece know of their coming, so when the door was flung open by a young man in his shirt sleeves, Isobel said baldly: 'Good afternoon, I've brought Mrs Olbinski to visit her niece.'

For a moment he started and stared at her in utter surprise. 'Aunty Ethel...here? How did she get here, then?'

'Dr Winter fetched her from Poland.'

He smiled then. 'Well, I'll be jiggered—wait till I tell Ma!' He suited the action to the word and bellowed over his shoulder, 'Where is she, then?'

'In the car. She can't walk very well—if you could carry her inside...?'

And from then on it was excited greetings, endless

cups of strong tea, neighbours popping in and a glass of port all round to mark the occasion.

It was difficult to prise Nanny loose from her family, and only then with the promise that they would come again the next day—'and we'll have a proper tea for you Aunty, and Nurse here.'

It was obvious to Isobel that this was to be the pattern of their days until she left, and since the doctor made no objection, she drove each afternoon to Peckham Rye and after a splendid tea and endless talk, drove back again. By the time the doctor got back in the evening, Nanny was once more in her dressing gown, sitting in her easy chair, waiting for her supper.

It made a long day, not that there was much to do, but Nanny liked to talk, which slowed up dressing and meals considerably, so that Isobel had little time alone. In the evenings when she would have loved an hour or so to herself, she had dinner with Dr Winter, who while not talking overmuch, expected her presence at his table. He asked about Nanny, of course, and visited her each day, but seemed preoccupied, Isobel thought, not exactly worried, but weighing the pros and cons about something or other. Perhaps he was worried about a patient; if it hadn't been for his austere expression she might have been tempted to ask. It wasn't until her week was half over that he observed during the soup: 'Well, you haven't much to say for yourself, have you?'

Tired, she thought, and peevish with it. She said soothingly, 'It seemed to me that you didn't want to

talk, so I didn't. And if you'd rather be alone do say
so. I don't mind a bit having my dinner somewhere
else—I could always have a tray with Nanny; she
likes company…'

'Meaning that I don't.' He sounded savage.

'Certainly not,' she said reasonably. 'And if you
stopped to think, you'd realise what a silly thing to
say that was.'

He looked at her with interest. 'And what exactly
do you mean by that, Isobel?'

'Well, you come back from a day's work, glad to
get away from patients and hospitals and illness; the
last person you want to see is someone who reminds
you of all those things…'

'So what do you suggest I do?' His smile was
mocking and amused.

She ignored that. 'Go out to dinner, or have someone to dine with you—someone like Miss Ella
Stokes.'

'And she'll guarantee me a delightful evening?'
His voice was silky.

'I should think so; she's so very pretty and she
makes you laugh…'

'And you don't?'

Isobel shook her head. 'No.' She added thoughtfully, 'Not that kind of laughing.'

He didn't answer that. Presently he said: 'I spoke
to Carl on the phone today—they send you their love.
They hope they'll see you again one day.'

'I liked them; I'd love to see them again, but of course I'm not likely to.'

He raised his eyebrows. 'Do you not care to travel, Isobel?'

'Well, of course I do, but I don't get many chances; I shan't forget these last two weeks.'

He examined the dish of vegetables being offered to him and didn't look at her. 'Neither shall I.' And when Gibson had left the room: 'Have you a boyfriend, Isobel?'

The question was so unexpected that she just sat and goggled at him until presently she managed: 'No, I've never had one. I'm not likely to either.'

'Why not?'

'I'm plain,' she pointed out patiently, 'you can see that for yourself. Even if I weren't I don't have much chance to meet people—men...'

Gibson came back into the room to clear the plates and hand the pudding, and when he had gone again she said composedly: 'If I'm to leave here on the day after tomorrow, would you mind if I telephoned the agency in the morning? So that if there's another case I can take it at once.'

'Why not give yourself a few days' break?' he asked perfunctorily.

'This case has been a very easy one, Dr Winter— I don't need a break.'

'You don't mind if we have our coffee here? I have some work to do. You take the next case that comes along, never mind where it is?'

'Well, yes.'

'So very soon Nanny will become a vague memory.'

She handed him his cup. 'No, she won't. I like Nanny very much, I'm going to miss her and I'll not forget her.'

'But you'll forget me?' he asked blandly.

'You haven't been my patient, Dr Winter.'

'You haven't answered my question, Isobel.' He gave her a small mocking smile, but she didn't smile back at him. Of course she wouldn't forget him; he was going to be with her for the rest of her life, in her dreams, beneath her eyelids when she closed her eyes, reflected in every mirror, his voice in her ear— and what a time to discover that! With him sitting opposite her, watching her like a hawk—and how could she have been in love with him and never known it until that moment?

She looked at him steadily, her face composed. 'No, I shan't forget you, Dr Winter. We shared quite an exciting week—at least, it was exciting for me.'

He nodded unsmiling. 'I think I might say the same. It only remains for me to thank you for your help, Isobel. And now, if you'll excuse me…'

She got up too, said goodnight quietly and went up to her room. It was a little too soon to settle Nanny for the night and she was glad of half an hour to herself.

It was going to be difficult, going away knowing that she would never see him again, but it was something she would have to face up to. She had had schoolgirl crushes, even supposed herself in love with a young houseman at the hospital where she had trained, but she knew that she loved Thomas Winter with a depth of feeling that wasn't going to be dismissed lightly. Even if she never set eyes on him again, it would make no difference to her love. It was just as well, she reminded herself sensibly, that he didn't like her very much.

Nanny was tired and a bit crotchety, so Isobel drew up a chair to the bed, picked up the book the old lady had been reading, and offered to read to her until she felt sleepy. It was a simple romantic story in which the girl was quite obviously going to marry the man before the last page, and Nanny listened avidly, so that when Isobel paused before the final chapter she was told in no uncertain terms to read that too.

'I'll sleep better if I know the pair of them are to wed,' declared Nanny.

So Isobel read on, glad that the final chapter was a short one. She read the satisfactory finish with a faint wistfulness; real life wasn't like that, at least not for her. But Nanny gave a happy sigh. 'That's how it should be,' she declared, 'a nice happy ending for each and every soul in love. And it's time you were wed, Isobel.'

'Isobel is wedded to her work,' said Dr Winter from the door, 'and you aren't asleep, Nanny. Why?'

Isobel laid the book down and got to her feet. 'I'll

come back presently,' she murmured, and made for the door, to be turned back by a firm hand.

'No need, I've only come to say goodnight to Nanny, and you may as well stay and hear what I have to say.'

He went and sat on the old lady's bed and picked up a knotted hand. 'I'm going away for a couple of days,' he told her, 'but I'll be back the day after to-morrow—in the late evening. Isobel is leaving us that morning, but Mrs Gibson will look after you, my dear, and Gibson will take you for a drive in the af-ternoon.'

Nanny looked into his face. 'You're very good to me, Mr Thomas, and it's lovely to be among old friends.' She gave a little cough. 'I'm sorry Isobel's going, but of course she has other patients, I daresay.' She presented a cheek for his kiss. 'I'll see you in two days' time, then.'

He got up and went to the door; his 'goodnight, Isobel', was impersonal and he didn't look at her for more than a second. When he had gone she went over to the bed and saw at once that Nanny was crying.

'But the doctor will be back in no time at all,' she comforted her, and Nanny said quite fiercely: 'That's not why I'm crying, my dear.' She dried her eyes. 'I'm going to sleep now, so you can say goodnight.'

Isobel went to bed too and hardly slept a wink, and just as she was dropping off wearily at six o'clock, Nanny called.

'I'm parched for a nice cup of tea,' she said. 'I

know it's early, but would it be bothering you to boil a kettle—you could have a cup with me.'

So Isobel crept downstairs, the house silent around her, and went along to the kitchen and made tea. She was carrying the tray across the hall when the study door opened and Dr Winter came out, so that she stopped rather suddenly and cried: 'My goodness, you gave me a fright!' And then: 'It's tea for Nanny.'

'Hasn't she slept?'

'Oh yes.'

His eyes searched her face, rather pale from sleeplessness and wreathed around by a cloud of mousy hair. 'But you haven't.'

She wondered why he was there, shaved and dressed ready for the day, and then remembered that he was going away. If she hadn't come down for the tea she would never have seen him. 'You're going away,' she said. 'You weren't going to say goodbye.' She added matter-of-factly: 'Of course, there's no earthly reason why you should. I hope you have a— a nice time.'

He didn't answer her but took the tray and set it on a nearby table. 'You feel I should have wished you goodbye, Isobel? By all means let us do the thing properly, then.'

He caught her close and kissed her hard, set her free and said blandly: 'I didn't expect to see you again, Isobel.'

He stood looking at her for a moment, her face puffy from a bad night, her hair wild, her sensible

dressing gown bundled on anyhow, then he picked up
the tray and put it into her hands once more, and all
the while she stood speechless. It was only when he
said in an offhand way, 'That tea will get cold', that
she scuttled away and up the stairs, almost falling
over her own feet in her hurry to get away from him
as quickly as possible. He had thought so little of her
that he had intended leaving without a word of goodbye, and yet he had kissed her in such a fashion—it
had amused him to do so, perhaps, and he would forget all about it within an hour, whereas she would
have to remember it for the rest of her life.

The day, begun so early, seemed to be twice its
usual length. Isobel took Nanny to Peckham Rye,
played cards with her until she was ready for bed and
then went to bed herself. She had packed her few
things, received her wages; an envelope with her
name scrawled upon it in Dr Winter's fierce hand-
writing and nothing but a cheque inside, and telephoned her mother to expect her during the next afternoon. There was nothing more to be done now; fate
couldn't be altered.

Gibson drove her back home, assuring her that it
had been the doctor's orders that he should do so, and
Isobel was glad of it for what with Nanny's tearful
goodbyes, and Mrs Gibson's regretful farewell, not to
mention those of the housemaid, the daily help and
the old man who did odd jobs and kept the small,
delightfully colourful garden behind the house in ap-
ple-pie order, she was feeling tearful herself. And at

the house even Gibson's controlled features relaxed as he wished her goodbye. 'We shall all miss you, Nurse,' he assured her. 'It's been a pleasure to have you in the house.'

She smiled mistily at him. 'Oh, Gibson, I've been so happy there!'

Her mother opened the front door then and she shot inside, afraid that she would blot her copybook by bursting into tears in the street.

Her mother kissed her, ignored her watery looks and said briskly: 'I've just made the tea. I expect you made some good friends at Dr Winter's, didn't you? What an unusual case it was, going all that way to fetch Mrs Olbinski. I hope Dr Winter thanked you properly.'

Isobel sat down in one of the shabby armchairs. She remembered vividly how he had kissed her and went a little pale. She said: 'Oh, yes. He's away from home now.' She mustered a smile. 'I shall miss Nanny—she had such a sharp tongue, but she was an old dear. I've been paid too—we'll go to the bank tomorrow and then I'll go along to the agency...'

Mrs Barrington poured the tea. 'Not even one day off, darling? You do need time to relax, you know.'

'Well, I thought I'd have tomorrow free; get my clothes sorted out and wash the smalls, and I'll take you out to lunch.'

'That will be lovely, darling, and now tell me all about your trip—I've always wanted to go to Stockholm...'

The agency, when Isobel called the next day, were able to offer her a new case on the following day— a well known film actress, the agency lady told her, and mentioned a name Isobel had never heard of, suffering most regrettably from mumps.

'You've had them, of course?' asked the agency lady, fixing Isobel with a sharp eye, and relaxed when she said she had. 'It shouldn't be a long case, Miss Barrington—you'll be expected to live in, of course. She has a studio flat somewhere off the Brompton Road.' She smiled frostily. 'Dr Winter was very satisfied with your services. I can't say that we were altogether pleased with the way in which he handled the financial side of it, but he's too valuable a client to argue with.' The smile was switched off. 'You will take the case, Miss Barrington?'

'Oh, yes,' said Isobel; a film actress, even with mumps, might help to take her mind off Thomas Winter.

It hadn't helped at all, Isobel admitted as she got wearily into bed at the end of her first day at Miranda le Creux's flat. If her own small shabby home had seemed cramped after the doctor's spacious home, Miranda's seemed even worse. Not that it was small—the rooms were large and lofty—but stuffed so full of flounced dressing tables, over-stuffed chairs, white rugs thick and shaggy enough to lose one's feet in, extravagantly draped curtains half covering net ruffles over the windows, and blown-up photos of Miranda in every conceivable position, that there was

OFFICIAL OPINION POLL

Dear Reader,

Since you are a book enthusiast, we would like to know what you think.

Inside you will find a short Opinion Poll. Please participate in our poll by sharing your opinion on 3 subjects that are very important to all of us.

To thank you for your participation, we would like to send you your choice of **2 FREE BOOKS** and a **FREE GIFT!**

Please enjoy them with our compliments.

Sincerely,

Pam Powers

Editor

P.S. Don't forget to indicate which books you prefer so we can send your FREE gifts today!

What's your pleasure...

Romance?

Enjoy **2 FREE BOOKS** that will fuel your imagination with intensely moving stories about life, love and relationships.

(OR)

Suspense?

Enjoy **2 FREE BOOKS** that will thrill you with a spine-tingling blend of suspense and mystery.

Whichever category you select, your **2 FREE BOOKS** have a combined cover price of $11.98 or more in the U.S. and $13.98 or more in Canada.

Simply place the sticker next to your preferred choice of books, complete the poll on the right page and you'll automatically receive **2 FREE BOOKS** and a **FREE GIFT** with no obligation to purchase anything!

We'll send you a wonderful surprise gift, *ABSOLUTELY FREE*, just for trying our books! Don't miss out — **MAIL THE REPLY CARD TODAY!**

Order online at
www.FreeBooksandGift.com

YOUR OPINION POLL
THANK-YOU FREE GIFTS INCLUDE

▶ **2 ROMANCE OR 2 SUSPENSE BOOKS**

▶ **A LOVELY SURPRISE GIFT**

DETACH AND MAIL CARD TODAY!

OFFICIAL OPINION POLL

YOUR OPINION COUNTS!

Please check TRUE or FALSE below to express your opinion about the following statements:

Q1 Do you believe in "true love"?

"TRUE LOVE HAPPENS ONLY ONCE IN A LIFETIME."　　○ TRUE　○ FALSE

Q2 Do you think marriage has any value in today's world?

"YOU CAN BE TOTALLY COMMITTED TO SOMEONE WITHOUT BEING MARRIED."　　○ TRUE　○ FALSE

Q3 What kind of books do you enjoy?

"A GREAT NOVEL MUST HAVE A HAPPY ENDING."　　○ TRUE　○ FALSE

Place the sticker next to one of the selections below to receive your 2 **FREE BOOKS** and **FREE GIFT**. I understand that I am under no obligation to purchase anything as explained on the back of this card.

Romance

193 MDL EE4P

393 MDL EE5D

Suspense

192 MDL EE4Z

392 MDL EE5P

0074823　**FREE GIFT CLAIM #** 3622

FIRST NAME　　　　LAST NAME

ADDRESS

APT.#　　　CITY

STATE/PROV.　　ZIP/POSTAL CODE　　(TF-SS-06)

The Reader Service — Here's How It Works:

Accepting your 2 free books and gift places you under no obligation to buy anything. You may keep the books and gift and return the shipping statement marked "cancel." If you do not cancel, about a month later we'll send you 3 additional books and bill you just $5.24 each in the U.S., or $5.74 each in Canada, plus 25¢ shipping & handling per book and applicable taxes if any.* That's the complete price, and — compared to cover prices of $5.99 or more each in the U.S. and $6.99 or more each in Canada — it's quite a bargain! You may cancel at any time, but if you choose to continue, every month we'll send you 3 more books, which you may either purchase at the discount price...or return to us and cancel your subscription.

*Terms and prices subject to change without notice. Sales tax applicable in N.Y.
Canadian residents will be charged applicable provincial taxes and GST.

If offer card is missing write to: The Reader Service, 3010 Walden Ave., P.O. Box 1867, Buffalo NY 14240-1867

BUSINESS REPLY MAIL
FIRST-CLASS MAIL   PERMIT NO. 717-003   BUFFALO, NY

POSTAGE WILL BE PAID BY ADDRESSEE

THE READER SERVICE
3010 WALDEN AVE
PO BOX 1341
BUFFALO NY 14240-8571

NO POSTAGE
NECESSARY
IF MAILED
IN THE
UNITED STATES

hardly room to turn round. Isobel discovered her patient lying in a king-size bed with a brocade headboard and a fur coverlet. Probably a very pretty girl, if the photos were to be believed, but just now with swollen jaws which turned her into a caricature of herself. Isobel felt instant sympathy, cooled, however, by her reception.

'There you are!' exclaimed Miss le Creux. 'I hope you know your work. I've never felt so ill in all my life, and Dr Martin actually dared to laugh at me this morning! It's vital that I get well quickly—I've landed a super modelling job in Cyprus. You'll have to do something about it.'

'I expect the doctor will have you well soon enough—mumps make you feel rotten, but they're soon over.' Isobel spoke with a calm certainty and her patient muttered, 'Oh, well, you'd better be right. You're not to let anyone in to see me. Nurse, there's a daily maid, Winnie—I've given her something to keep her mouth shut; and don't you dare tell anyone either.'

'I'm not in the habit of discussing my patients, Miss le Creux,' said Isobel gently. 'And now, since Doctor Martin is coming later on this morning, suppose you have a bath while I make the bed and tidy up?'

She had never known a patient make such a fuss. It wasn't as if Miss le Creux had a high temperature or a sore throat. Isobel thought of Nanny, tied in knots with arthritis and never complaining, and naturally her thoughts went straight to Thomas Winter; she thought of him lovingly and sadly, wondering what he would be doing and whether he had spared a single thought for her since she had left his house. She was sure he hadn't.

Miss le Creux shrieking from the bathroom brought her unhappy thoughts to a halt, and the rest of her day was taken up completely with ministering to that young lady's wants. She didn't need a nurse, Isobel decided sleepily as she climbed into her bed in the over-furnished room next to her patient's, but if she chose to have one and pay for it, that was her business. Isobel flung one of the fat frilled pillows on to the floor, her last waking thought predictably of Dr Winter. He would have had the mumps, she decided; he led the kind of well-ordered life which wouldn't tolerate anything likely to disrupt its smooth passage. He must have been a dear little boy. She wished she had asked Nanny about him, but that would have been a gross impertinence. Perhaps it was as well that she didn't know too much about him, she might forget him all the sooner.

As the slow week crawled towards its end, she wondered just how long it took to forget someone you loved—well, forget wasn't the right word; she would never forget him, but somehow or other she had to push him out of sight at the back of her mind. Only he wouldn't go. He popped up at the oddest times, especially when Miss le Creux was being extra tire-some and she found herself longing to drop everything and leave the flat. She couldn't do that, of course. Bobby's school fees loomed on the horizon, and they were an ever-present spur to work, but she longed foolishly for the weeks to roll back, so that she might find herself in Dr Winter's house, looking at the portraits on the walls and then watching the door open as he came into the elegant room.

It was half way through the second week before Dr Martin assured his patient that there was no reason at all which should prevent her getting out into the fresh air and resuming a normal life. 'You're not ill, young lady,' he boomed at her. 'The sooner you go out and about, the sooner your face will resume its normal proportions.' A remark which sent Miss le Creux to the nearest mirror to give her lovely, empty face a close examination.

'Do I sag?' she demanded of Isobel. 'What did he mean? I won't have my career ruined!'

Isobel paused in her endless tidying after her patient had dragged herself out of her bed. 'You look perfectly all right to me,' she said tartly. 'I can think of lots of actresses, famous ones, who aren't in the least pretty. I don't know what you're worrying about.'

'Of course you don't,' snapped Miss le Creux, 'how could you possibly? You're so plain you don't need to worry about your face at all. But I suppose that doesn't matter to you—nurses are supposed to be wedded to their work, aren't they?' She gave a little titter and turned back to the mirror. 'I must say you've been quite nice; I suppose I must take Dr Martin's advice and get around a bit. Your week's up in two days, isn't it? You might as well go tomorrow. I suppose I settle up with the agency?'

'Yes, I'm afraid they'll expect you to pay for the full week even if I leave a day earlier.'

Miss le Creux turned astonished blue eyes on her. 'Like hell they will! But I shouldn't worry, my boyfriend will see to all that anyway. Do I have to tip you?'

'No,' said Isobel stonily. Miranda le Creux might be very pretty, she might even be talented, but she had what Isobel's mother would have called no background. True, most patients gave their nurse some small gift when they left, but it was given with gratitude and accepted in the spirit in which it was given, and it certainly wasn't expected. She suddenly wanted to leave as soon as possible and be sent to a case where she really had to nurse someone who needed nursing. She went along to the kitchen to ask Winnie for her patient's morning coffee, her heart so full of longing for Thomas Winter that her chest felt as though it might burst. It was lovely to go down the stairs of the block of flats where Miranda le Creux lived and through the entrance door into the street and know that she was free of the tiresome girl and her dreadful flat. Isobel nipped smartly to the nearest bus stop and set off for home. She would have to ring the agency when she got there and tell them she had left and find out about another case, but at least she would have the rest of the day, perhaps longer.

Her mother was in the garden, hanging up the washing with Blossom gavotting round her feet. She put the clothes pegs down at once as soon as she saw Isobel and said happily: 'Hullo darling, are you back for good, or is this a day off?'

'For good, thank heavens.' Isobel whisked Blossom on to her shoulder. 'Gosh, it's nice to be here!'

'We'll have coffee—oh, there's a parcel for you— quite a small one. It came three days ago, but you said not to send anything on...'

It was quite small, square and neatly wrapped, and her name and address were typed on a label. Isobel turned it over several times and then unwrapped it slowly. The box inside was leather, and when she opened it there was an amber necklace carefully coiled inside on the velvet. There was a card inside written in Dr Winter's fierce hand. 'To Isobel, with my thanks.' It was signed T. W.

'How charming,' observed Mrs Barrington, peering over Isobel's shoulder. 'The necklace, I mean—and what a businesslike little note.'

'Well, he didn't like me very much, Mother,' said Isobel soberly.

'So why this really lovely amber necklace?'

Isobel touched it with a gentle finger. The day they had taken Nanny out for a drive they had stopped in Sopot and looked in a small shop tucked away in one of the side streets. The necklace had been in its window and she had admired it. And he had bought it, but perhaps not for her; she would never know that. 'I must write and thank him,' she said quietly, and closed the box, then because she knew that her mother was looking at her thoughtfully, added brightly: 'Amber's very common in Poland, you know. I believe you can buy it in most of the Baltic countries. It will look very nice with that brown dress...'

'It'll look lovely with your blue—I should wear it, darling, not put it away in a drawer.'

So Isobel put on the blue dress and the amber necklace and that evening composed a stiff little note of thanks. She had no idea that it would be so hard to write to someone you loved who didn't love you, without letting them see how she felt. It reached the doctor the following morning, and he read it several times with an inscrutable face and then put it carefully in his pocket.

There was another case for Isobel when she rang the agency—an elderly man living in Hampstead; a heart failure, too ill to be moved, and perhaps she wouldn't mind going along that evening, suggested the agency lady. A car would be sent for her at nine o'clock. Isobel hesitated; she had planned to have a day at home and was on the point of saying so when the voice at the other end said: 'It'll be a very short case, Miss Barrington—perhaps only a day or possibly two at the most.'

So she packed her case once more and when an elderly chauffeur-driven car drew up outside the front door, she said goodbye to her mother and got in. The chauffeur was elderly too, and since she had got in beside him, he was willing to talk, so by the time that they had reached the house, she knew that her patient was over eighty, a widower with a scattered family, a faithful but elderly housekeeper, the chauffeur and a couple of daily helps. 'So we're all at sixes and sevens,' said the chauffeur, 'Mrs Wills not being that young any more, as you might say, and the two women who come in not knowing what to do. Doctor said we'd have to have a nurse straight away. Did you count on staying up all night, miss?'

'No, but I can,' said Isobel bracingly. 'I'm just back from an easy case and I'm not tired.' She peered out. 'Is this it?'

They had entered a short drive and stopped before a massive Edwardian brick villa, very ugly and very solid. Isobel got out of the car and mounted the wide steps to its massive front door.

Twelve hours later she was going down them again. The agency lady had been right; the case had been a very short one.

'Bed for you, darling,' said her mother when she walked into her home, blue eyes wide in a face white with a sleepless night. 'And what's more,' went on Mrs Barrington, 'you're having a day off tomorrow.' She added cunningly: 'The garden wants weeding and the kitchen curtains need washing, and you know I can't get at them.'

It was pleasant to be home, pottering around the

house and tiny garden, playing with Blossom, and since it was a lovely warm day, taking down the kitchen curtains, washing and ironing them, and as there was time before tea, climbing rather precariously on to the stepladder to hang them up again. She was half way through this task when her mother called from the chair by the sitting room window.

'Do we know anyone with a Rolls-Royce, darling?'

Isobel stretched across the window to insert a hook. 'Only that friend of Father's, years ago—Mr... Oh, lord, Dr Winter's got one!' She stuck in another hook and raised her voice so that her mother would hear her in the other room. 'But he's the last person to come here.' She leaned over a little further and inserted the last hook, and then in sudden panic cried, 'Mother, if it's him, I'm not here...'

Too late, of course. He was at the kitchen door, making the little room smaller than it already was. She perched on the top step, watching him, not speaking for the simple reason that her heart was thumping so madly that breathing had become difficult.

He didn't waste time over social niceties. 'Nanny's got bronchitis, she wants you to look after her.'

Isobel forgot about being shy. 'Oh, the poor dear, is she bad? And just as she was doing so nicely too...' She looked at him properly then; she hadn't gone higher than his tie when he had come in. He looked stern and angry as well and his eyes were like granite; she thought it very likely that he had come against his will because Nanny had insisted. She said kindly in her gentle voice, 'I'm indeed sorry to hear about Nanny, but I can't come, you know; I go where the agency sends me and I'm only just back from a case. I'm sure if you phone them they'll have a nurse free…'

He gave her a thin smile. 'My dear Isobel, you underestimate me. I have already arranged with the agency that you'll return with me this evening.'

Her eyes grew round. 'The arrogance of it!' she declared. 'I may refuse a case, you know, Dr Winter, and I'm doing just that!' Her voice spiralled into a squeak as he reached up and lifted her off the steps and set her down gently, his hands still on her shoulders.

'You won't do that,' his voice was quiet, 'you're a kind girl, and gentle. I'm sorry if I've made you angry, but Nanny is ill, and I haven't brought her all this way to see her slip through my fingers.'

Isobel, very conscious of his hands, conscious too that for him this was a handsome apology, smiled at him. 'I'll need half an hour to collect my things. Do you want me to come with you or shall I come later?'

Before he could reply Mrs Barrington spoke from the door where she had been shamelessly eavesdropping. 'While you get your things together I'll make tea—you'll have a cup, Dr Winter, and one of the scones Isobel made this morning?'

He dropped his hands from Isobel's shoulders. 'Indeed I will, Mrs Barrington. Your daughter's cooking was one of the high spots of our trip.'

'Then come into the sitting-room,' invited Mrs Barrington, 'and I'll put the kettle on. How long will Isobel be with you?'

He opened his mouth to say something and then bit it back. 'A week, two perhaps,' he said suavely. 'It's hard to tell at this stage. Nanny is elderly and tired.'

Isobel had gone, he sat on the edge of the kitchen table while Mrs Barrington filled the kettle and put it on the old-fashioned gas stove. The scones were on a plate on the table and he took one and ate it.

'Exquisite,' he said, and took another, and Mrs Barrington, her back to him, putting cups and saucers on a tray, said: 'Yes, it's eighteenth-century Bow, it belonged to my mother.'

'Actually,' said the doctor, and his voice sounded surprisingly young, 'I was talking about the scones, not the plate.'

Mrs Barrington turned round to look at him. She said softly: 'She's such a dear girl.'

He stared back at her, his dark eyes gleaming. 'Yes, I've discovered that, Mrs Barrington.'

They were embarked on their tea, chatting cosily, by the time Isobel got downstairs again. 'I've packed enough for a week,' she said to no one in particular, and looked with surprise at the almost empty plate.

'I had no lunch,' said the doctor meekly.

They left shortly afterwards, Isobel very neat in uniform; she was wearing the amber necklace under it. She didn't think that the slight bulge it made showed.

'I have to go out as soon as I get back home,' said Dr Winter, 'so listen carefully now so that I don't have to say it all over again.' He embarked on a brief résumé of Nanny's illness, her treatment, medicines, diet and condition. When he'd finished he asked briefly: 'Well, have you got all that? I'll leave a phone number where I can be reached if you're worried, but don't do that unless you have to.'

He didn't seem the same man who had sat not half an hour since discussing the beauties of Coalport china with her mother, devouring her scones like a hungry wolf. He was abstracted now, coolly impersonal, his voice as cool as his manner. She wondered where he was going that evening that could be so important that she was only to phone him in a dire emergency. That beastly girl, probably. Isobel turned her head away and stared out of the window. She had been silly to come, opening a wound that hadn't yet begun to heal.

But she forgot that when she saw Nanny. The old lady was sitting up high against her pillows. She looked small and frail and very tired, but she smiled when she saw Isobel and took her small capable hand and put it to her cheek.

'You naughty old thing,' said Isobel softly, 'but don't worry, we'll have you well again in no time. Just let me go along to my room for a moment, then we'll spend a cosy evening together and you'll eat your supper and go to sleep.'

'I can't sleep,' said Nanny peevishly.

'Yes, you can. I'll sit here until you do.'

The old eyes peered at her. 'You will?' She stopped to cough. 'I'm not scared, only...'

'I know, Nanny, and if you wake in the night, one squeak from you and I'll be here—I'm only in the next room with the door open.'

Dr Winter came in then; he had changed into a dinner jacket and her heart almost stopped at the sight of him. No man had any right to be as good-looking as he was. She gave him a chilly look. 'If you're going to be here for a moment, Dr Winter, I'll go and see Mrs Gibson about Nanny's supper...'

She didn't wait for his answer and when she got back he was on the point of leaving. 'I'm already late,' he told her austerely, just as though it were her fault.

There was a lot to do for Nanny. The attack had come on dreadfully suddenly, and although Mrs Gibson had done her best, Nanny had been fretful and difficult. It would be a day or two before the antibiotics would take effect, in the meantime it was just a question of good nursing—a ceaseless round of cool drinks, pillows shaken, sheets smoothed, bedbaths and nourishment taken however unwillingly. Isobel settled her patient for the night finally and with Mrs Gibson taking her place for half an hour, had her supper, bathed, got into her nightie and dressing gown and went back to Nanny's room. The old lady was indeed poorly, but once she could be got to sleep it would help matters. Isobel listened to Mrs Gibson's whispered offer of a tray of sandwiches and a thermos in case she was kept up late, wished her goodnight and turned her attention to Nanny.

The old lady was wide awake, feverish and inclined to talk a lot. So Isobel pulled up a chair close to the bed, took a hand in hers, and listened while Nanny rambled on about her life in Poland. 'Such a waste, if I've come all this way home—I might just as well have stayed in Gdansk and saved Mr Thomas the trouble.'

'You're wrong there,' said Isobel. 'The doctor—Mr Thomas is lonely, I think. He really needs you, Nanny…'

'What he needs,' said Nanny weakly, 'is a wife and children.'

'Then he'd need you even more.' Isobel turned a pillow deftly. 'You simply have to get well as quickly as possible, Nanny.'

'Yes, dear, I'll do my best.'

'Well, that's more like it. I'm going to give you your antibiotic and a warm drink and then you're going to close your eyes, Nanny, and I promise I'll stay here until you're asleep. If you wake in the night you only have to call.'

It didn't take long, with Nanny settled against her pillows, her eyes resolutely shut, Isobel made a note of her temperature—down a little, she was glad to see—made sure that she had everything handy for the night and sat down again, tucking the old hands on the coverlet into her own. She reckoned she would be there for an hour or so yet; Nanny, despite her cough medicine, was coughing a lot. But presently she nodded off into a light doze, only to wake in a little while and ask querulously what the time was. 'And you ought to be in bed,' she added.

'I've had a lazy day at home and I'm not a bit tired. Go to sleep again, Nanny dear. You're going to feel better in the morning.'

So Nanny dozed off again and this time she slept through Mrs Gibson's soundless entrance with a tray and her whispered: 'You'll be all right, Nurse? The doctor said we'd best get to bed early—we were up most of the night and it's been a long day.'

'I'm fine, Mrs Gibson. Have a good sleep, and goodnight.'

The house was very quiet. Presumably Gibson had gone to his bed too and the doctor would let himself in. Mrs Gibson had left the door open and Isobel could see the faint glow of a light in the hall. She stifled a yawn and decided to wait another half hour and make sure that Nanny was sleeping properly.

Before the half hour was up, Nanny had roused again, demanding a drink, wanting to know the time once more, complaining of being hot. Isobel dealt with everything with quiet speed, persuaded Nanny to have another pill, assured her that she would sleep again, and sat down once more.

'Hold my hand,' said Nanny and this time she slept deeply. Isobel waited a little while; it was almost one o'clock and she longed for her bed. She was on the point of loosening the old lady's hand from hers when she heard the faint sound of the door being shut downstairs. Dr Winter was home again. Presently she heard him coming upstairs. He trod quietly, but he was a big man and the stairs creaked a little. He came just as quietly into the room, went straight to beside the bed and looked at Nanny and then at Isobel, sitting there with her hair hanging round her face, and that pinched with tiredness. 'Go to bed!' His whisper was so harsh that she stared at him, wondering what she had done to make him angry.

'Nanny has only just gone to sleep,' she whispered back. 'I promised I'd stay with her until she slept.' She nodded towards the notes on the side table. 'Her temp's down, so is her pulse.'

'Good. Now do as I say. Goodnight!' His whisper was worse than a loud angry voice, the furious look he turned on her made her insides cold. She got up from her chair and went out of the room without a word. In the morning she would ask him what was wrong. She tumbled into bed and was asleep in an instant.

CHAPTER SIX

ISOBEL WAS up again soon after five o'clock, dealing with Nanny's cough, giving her a hot drink, more medicine, sponging her face and hands. She went away to dress when Mrs Gibson came, and have a quick breakfast before setting about getting her patient comfortable again. The old lady was sitting up, looking decidedly brighter when Dr Winter arrived. He bade Isobel a brief good morning, examined Nanny, pronounced her to be progressing nicely, rang the bell and when Gibson answered it, requested that Mrs Gibson should come to the room, and when that good lady had presented herself, asked her to keep Nanny company for a short time. 'And you, Isobel, will come to my study, if you would be so good.'

She followed him without a word; at least she would have the opportunity to ask him why he had been so angry in the early hours of that morning. He opened the study door for her and she went past him and at his invitation sat down. He sat himself behind his desk, and before he could speak, she plunged in, anxious to get it over with.

'I made you angry last night,' she said levelly, 'and I think I should be told why; if it's something I've done wrong, I'm sorry, though I can't for the life of me think what it could be…' She added in a reason-able voice: 'I expect that's why you wanted to see me.'

'I wanted to see you, but for a different reason—to apologise for speaking as I did last night. I wasn't angry with you, Isobel, but with myself for leaving you here in my house, to all intents and purposes alone with a sick old woman when you should have been asleep in your bed.'

'Oh, that's quite wrong,' said Isobel bracingly. 'That's what I'm here for—I'm used to sitting up till all hours and I don't mind being alone. Why, you might just as well blame yourself for leaving the maids to wash up after you've had a meal. You pay them for doing it, they work for you. Well, you pay me and I work for you too.' She smiled a little and her eyes twinkled. 'It's no good keeping a dog and barking yourself, you know.'

He laughed then. 'I've never met a girl with so much common sense,' he told her, a remark which she hoped was a compliment, although no girl wanted to be complimented on common sense; a pretty face or lovely eyes or beautiful hair, but what did common sense ever do for a girl?

She got to her feet. 'Oh, well, if that's all, I'll get back to Nanny.'

The doctor stood up too. 'I've arranged with Mrs Gibson to be with Nanny for two hours each after-noon so that you may go out if you wish, and I shall be at home for the next few nights, so there'll be no need for you to sit with Nanny once you've settled her for the night. I'll look in on her from time to time and call you if necessary.'

Isobel shook her head. 'That won't do at all,' she observed calmly. 'You work all day like the rest of us.'

He went to the door and opened it. 'You will allow me to arrange things as I wish, Isobel.' She had heard that silky tone before; she didn't dispute it now. She said quietly: 'Yes, of course, Dr Winter,' and slipped past him, back to Nanny's room.

There wasn't much improvement in Nanny during the day, but Isobel hadn't expected it. It was enough that she was holding her own and not getting worse. 'You're getting better,' Isobel encouraged her. 'Another day or two and I expect Dr Winter will let your niece come and see you.'

The old lady brightened at the prospect. 'Now that would be fine. I'd like to show her how grand I am— it's a pity my poor Stan isn't alive to see me too.'

'Wouldn't he be glad to see you living here with all your old friends?' observed Isobel cheerfully. 'Now, what do you fancy for lunch?'

The day wore on and when the doctor came home he went straight to Nanny's room. 'You're better,' he said at once, and after he'd gone over her chest and pronounced an improvement: 'You went out, Isobel?'

'Yes, thank you. It was a lovely afternoon, I went along to the park.'

He nodded. 'Good. Take the car if you want to go

to your home, although it would be better for you if
you took some exercise.'

She gave him a limpid look. Her days were hardly
idle; to sit with her feet up in the sun would do nicely.
She said: 'Yes, Dr Winter,' in a mild voice which
caused him to give her one of his hard stares.

'I shall be home for dinner, I hope you'll join me,
Isobel.'

She went downstairs presently, still in uniform, her
hair very neat under the white cap, wishing with all
her heart that she was in billowing silk and her hair
in one of those artless styles which took hours to
achieve. She would, of course, need another face to
go with that, in which case, she told herself sensibly,
she might just as well keep the one she'd got.

She had come downstairs quietly, but the doctor
had the ears of a hawk. 'In here,' he called from the
drawing-room, and as she pushed open the door
which was ajar: 'Have a drink, Isobel, I'm sure
you've earned it. Try some Madeira and tell me if
you like it.'

She sat down composedly on a small armchair and
sipped her wine. 'It's very…' she paused and finished
lamely: 'nice.' And when he didn't remark on that:
'Have you had a busy day, Dr Winter?'

'Very. I had quite a backlog, but I'm almost
through it. I want to be free for the weekend. I shall
be away.' He was watching her carefully. 'I'm going
down to Ella's home in Sussex.'

Isobel's heart gave a great leap and stopped, then

went on again very fast, but her face remained serene. 'Sussex is a charming county,' she offered pleasantly.

'Not your part of the world, though?' asked the doctor idly.

'Oh, no.' The Madeira was loosening her cautious tongue. 'But Berkshire is beautiful too.'

'Isn't that rather depending on which part of the county you're in? Can't say that I care for Reading...'

'Oh, we lived miles from there,' said Isobel. 'Hinton Bassett—it's a beautiful village and so quiet once the tourists have gone. We lived...' She stopped, aware suddenly that she was talking about herself and probably boring him.

'You lived?' prompted her companion.

'In the village,' she mumbled, and added: 'I think Madeira is a little strong.'

'You don't like it? Let me give you some sherry...'

She said hastily: 'Oh, no, thank you, I've almost finished it anyway.'

Dinner was a pleasant enough meal. Isobel, in her efforts to be nothing more than the nurse sent to help out for a week or so, leaned over backwards to be just that, and the doctor, wickedly plying her with his best claret, enjoyed himself very much, and when after they had had their coffee she excused herself on the grounds that Nanny would need to be tucked up for the night, he watched her go with real regret, wondering how he could possibly have found her rather dull when they had first met.

The days slipped away in a gentle routine, with

Nanny improving slowly but steadily. Isobel spent her afternoons in Kensington Gardens or peering in the windows of the smart boutiques, and once, when it was raining, in Harrods, prowling from one department to another, pretending that she could buy whatever she fancied. She got so carried away that she was very nearly late back.

Dr Winter she saw only briefly during the day, although each evening they had dinner together. She wished, a little wistfully, that he would invite her to stay after that meal and talk, for they had plenty to talk about at table, but he never did, getting up at once when she said she should go back to Nanny, opening the door for her and wishing her goodnight so smartly that she could only feel he was glad to see the back of her.

On Friday she asked Gibson if she was to have dinner downstairs. 'For the doctor will be away, won't he, and it seems a great waste to lay the table just for me. I could easily have a tray in the little room at the back of the hall.'

Gibson's features had relaxed in a smile. 'That wouldn't do, Nurse. Dr Winter would wish you to have your meals exactly as though he were here too.' He added: 'He'll be going about six o'clock, Nurse.'

The doctor had been to see Nanny in the morning. She was making real progress now and sitting out of bed for several hours, but she was tired and crotchety with it, and Isobel was hard put to it to keep her happy during the day. She was reading aloud to her patient when the doctor came home just after five o'clock. She stopped when he came in, put a finger in the page and waited patiently while he talked to Nanny, looked at her progress chart and then said: 'How would you like visitors tomorrow, Nanny?' He glanced at Isobel. 'A good idea, don't you think, Isobel? Nanny's niece could come to tea and stay for half an hour, and if she's not too tired, then one or two of the rest of her family can come—but only one at a time to start with.' He didn't wait for an answer but went away, to reappear after half an hour, dressed for the evening. 'Isobel, come downstairs, will you, I'll give you a number to ring if you should want me for any reason, and change the medicine too, I think.'

She followed him downstairs and into his study. 'Sit down,' he told her, and sat down himself to write on a pad. 'Now listen,' he began, 'I think we might make one or two changes...'

He was interrupted: the door was flung open and Ella came in, a vision in a sky blue suede skirt and a silk shirt, its sleeves carelessly rolled up, its buttons undone to what Isobel considered to be a quite indecent level, not that the effect wasn't devastating...

'Darling!' cried the vision. 'You're ready and I haven't had a minute to change, so I've brought everything with me, and I'll slip upstairs and dress now. Shall I use your room?'

'Certainly not.' It was impossible to tell from the doctor's manner if he was annoyed or not. 'Use one of the guest rooms—and be quiet, Nanny's resting and I don't want her disturbed.'

Ella wrinkled her nose at him. 'You grumpy old thing! I'm glad I'm not one of your patients.' She allowed her lovely eyes to rest on Isobel for a moment. 'Hullo, you back again?' She didn't waste time on her, though, but smiled enchantingly at the doctor, blew him a kiss and danced out of the room.

There was a brief silence after she had gone and then the doctor went on with what he had been saying just as though there had been no interruption. 'And I'll be back late on Sunday night—please leave a message on the hall table if there's anything worrying you.' He smiled briefly. 'That's all, thank you, Isobel.'

She went back to Nanny and found the old lady sitting up in bed, very peevish. 'That young madam's here, rattling around, banging doors, and I can hear the bath water somewhere…'

'It's not for long, Nanny. Miss Stokes is changing before they leave.'

'She'd better not come in here,' declared Nanny crossly, and added, 'Baggage!'

'Shall I read to you for a bit?' asked Isobel. 'It's too early to get your supper, isn't it? Or there's that show you like on the TV.'

'You read to me, my dear, you've got a nice soothing voice.'

So Isobel read—another simple love story with a happy ending; Nanny never tired of them. She had been reading for half an hour when the door was thrust open and Ella came in. This time she was in pink taffeta, with a long tight bodice and a very short full skirt. Her hair was piled up on top of her head and a pink scarf was twisted round it, and her shoes were mere scraps of gold kid on four-inch heels. 'How do I look?' she wanted to know, 'it's a bit *avant-garde*, but at least everyone will notice me.'

'You're not decent,' said Nanny with a snap.

'It's very unusual,' said Isobel mildly, anxious for Nanny not to get all worked up, 'but would you mind going away? Mrs Olbinski isn't allowed visitors.'

Ella shrugged. 'You make a fine pair!' her voice was a little shrill. 'I say, I've left my things in your room, will you go and pack them up? I'll have to take them with me.'

'No, I will not pack your things, Miss Stokes. I'm Mrs Olbinski's nurse, not your maid—and will you please go?' Isobel added gently: 'And leave my room tidy, won't you.'

Just for a moment she thought that Ella was going to hit her, but she turned on her ridiculous heels and went out, banging the door shut; even then Isobel could hear her raging as she went down the stairs. It was five minutes or more before Mrs Gibson poked her head round the door.

'I've tidied your room, Nurse—Miss Stokes had no reason to use it, there are rooms enough and to spare—messed up the bathroom too. I got Edith to get her things together and take them down to her.

They've gone now.' She glanced at Nanny. 'Shall I see about a nice supper for Nanny?'

'Thank you, Mrs Gibson.' Isobel smiled and spoke with her usual calm, although her hands were shaking. She hadn't met anyone quite like Ella Stokes before, and her mild nature had erupted into a fine temper she was struggling to subdue. She asked: 'Did the doctor hear any of the—the fuss here?'

Mrs Gibson shook her head. 'He was in the study telephoning. He only came into the hall as Miss Stokes went shouting downstairs, but she'd done that so often he didn't take much notice, only asked her to hush up.'

Nanny was sitting very upright against her pillows. 'It ought to have been you, Isobel…'

'Me, Nanny?'

'Yes, instead of that trumpery creature—going off for the weekend with Mr Thomas, I mean; he doesn't know a dear sweet girl when he sees her.' She nodded her head vigorously. 'A fine pair you'd make, and you're good for him too, especially when he gets a bit uppity.'

'Nanny, whatever are you talking about? Dr Winter and I haven't a thing in common…'

Nanny chuckled. 'You mark my words. Things aren't always what they seem, and as for that sauce-box, she'll find there's many a slip 'twixt cup and lip.'

Having delivered herself of these wise if unoriginal remarks, Nanny consented to lie back against her pillows once more, leaving Isobel to go down to the kitchen for her supper tray, her thoughts far away, whizzing down to Sussex, imagining Thomas and his Ella talking together. Ella would be witty and amusing and Thomas would laugh, something he so seldom did with herself. She sighed, received the creamed chicken Nanny fancied and bore it back upstairs to her patient. After supper she telephoned Nanny's niece and arranged to get her to come to tea on the next afternoon. 'Just for half an hour and a cup of tea,' she advised. 'Nanny's still not very well, but she'd love to see you.'

And that done, she went down to her solitary dinner. She had very little appetite, but Gibson seemed determined that she should enjoy the various dishes Mrs Gibson had prepared, so she ate her way obediently through seafood pancakes, lamb cutlets and an assortment of vegetables and a rich chocolate pudding which Gibson assured her had been made especially for her, seeing that she had enjoyed the last one Mrs Gibson had made.

'And I've put the coffee tray in the drawing room, Nurse,' he informed her. 'Nanny's quite comfortable and you can drink it in peace.'

The weekend passed peacefully enough. Nanny's niece, rendered tonguetied by the magnificence of the doctor's house, hardly spoke above a whisper and agreed eagerly to a return visit on the next day, and as for Nanny, she thoroughly enjoyed the visits, pointing out the great comfort with which she was being surrounded, describing the food, eulogising the doctor and, when she wasn't in the room, Isobel.

Her cough was almost gone, although she was tired out as a result of it and would take some time before she felt herself again. All the same, Isobel was content with her progress. Another week, she thought, and her services wouldn't be required any more.

She had settled Nanny for the night, had had her own dinner and was sitting in the drawing room with the coffee tray when the door opened and Dr Winter walked in.

Isobel put down her coffee cup, a delicate Sèvres trifle which tinkled against its saucer because her hand was shaking. 'Oh,' she said, 'you're not coming back until very late this evening,' and then blushed because it had been such a stupid thing to say.

'So I had thought, but circumstances dictated otherwise.' He went and sat down in the winged chair opposite hers and Gibson came noiselessly in with a tray of sandwiches and fresh coffee. He looked hungry, thought Isobel—no, not hungry, tired and, under the tiredness, angry. She said in her pleasant way, 'You're tired, I expect. I was going up to see if Nanny was all right anyway.'

But before she could get to her feet he said: 'No, don't go. I'm in no mood for talking, but you're restful.'

So she sat and watched him wolfing his sandwiches, but only when he lifted the now empty coffee pot to refill his cup did she say: 'You'd like more coffee—I'll ring,' and did so without waiting for him to reply. He didn't speak until he'd emptied most of the second pot too, and by then his face had resumed its habitual bland expression.

'I think Nanny is well enough to have a change of air; I'd like you to go with her, Isobel.'

She hadn't been expecting anything like that, and she looked up in surprise without speaking, waiting for him to explain.

'Do you know Suffolk at all? No? I have a cottage at Orford—it's a few miles from the sea—a smallish place and delightful at this time of year. Mrs Cobb, who lives nearby, will look after you and I'll arrange for a wheelchair for Nanny. You won't be bored. Yachts come in and go out to the North Sea, there's plenty to see.' He gave her a long look. 'Two weeks, Isobel?'

She said quietly: 'Yes, of course, Dr Winter.'

He nodded. 'Good. I'm thinking of having a holiday myself—perhaps you would stay here for another few weeks after you get back. I know there won't be much for you to do, but Nanny has taken a fancy to you and I want someone here with her.'

She said again: 'Very well, but I'd be glad if you could arrange for someone to take over once in a while so that I can go home. My brother starts his holidays soon, we hadn't planned to go away'—when had they ever had the money to go away?—'but we usually go somewhere for the day...'

'That will be arranged.' And then with sudden brusqueness: 'Don't let me keep you up.'

She wished him goodnight quietly, not much liking her summary dismissal but reasonable enough to realise that he was worried about something and most likely wanted to be alone. In any case, she pointed out to herself in her usual sensible manner, he had never sought her company; he had only asked her to stay so that he could tell her his plans for Nanny. In due course, she supposed, she would be told the details.

But not from him. It was Nanny, all agog after his visit to her the next morning, who supplied them.

'Many's the time I've been there,' she told an avidly listening Isobel. 'Each summer I'd take Mr Thomas down in June and his mother and father would come down later. Very nice it was too.'

'A cottage?' asked Isobel.

'Well, as you might say, there's cottages and cottages. Merman Cottage is bigger than most, I daresay. Mr Thomas says he'll arrange for the little sitting room downstairs to be fitted for me to make it easy. You don't mind coming with me?'

'I think it sounds great fun.'

'Well, I hope you'll stay for a few weeks yet. I know I'm better, but it's nice to have you around, so I told Mr Thomas, especially as he's going on holiday himself when we get back. The Far East he says, he wants to get right away.'

Probably with Ella, thought Isobel miserably.

Her mother, when she told her, was delighted, and made light of the fact that Isobel would probably not be home to see much of Bobby. 'You won't be gone all that time,' she pointed out, 'and his holidays are endless in the summer—besides, it's a good job, darling, and you won't have to go to that beastly agency every week or so. You go and enjoy yourself. I'm sure Dr Winter will arrange something so that you can see Bobby—a day off before you go or something…'

But the days slipped by and nothing was said. Nanny was up and dressed now, although still not quite herself, and soon the date was fixed for their departure. Isobel, picking over her scanty wardrobe for suitable clothes to take with her, since she wasn't to wear uniform, began to worry. Bobby would be home within the next day or so, and since the doctor never seemed to be at home, and when he was he was either in a hurry to go out, or went straight to his study and shut the door, she had managed only once to ask him if she might have a free day before they went to Orford.

He had frowned, glancing up only briefly from the letter he was reading. 'I said I would arrange something,' he told her, 'and I will do so.' But here it was on the eve of departure and not a word said. She had packed for Nanny and was busy piling clothes neatly into her own case when she put down the skirt she was folding and marched downstairs, only to find him actually at the door on his way out. His 'Yes?' was hardly encouraging, and then before she had managed to get a word out, 'I haven't forgotten, Isobel.' He was through the door and had shut it firmly while she was still staring at him.

And after that she wasn't going to say another word. She phoned her mother briefly in the morning to say that she wouldn't be home for a week or so and then went to get Nanny ready for their journey.

They were to be driven there and she had supposed Gibson was to do that, but when she followed the doctor with Nanny in his arms down the staircase and into the hall it was to find the Rolls at the door, their luggage in the boot and Gibson standing holding the door for them to get in. Nanny was stowed on to the back seat, wrapped around with rugs and cushions, but when Isobel prepared to get in beside her the doctor said: 'In front with me, Isobel.'

She got in, her temper ruffled enough for her to say tartly: 'You probably consider it a waste of time, Dr Winter, but ''would you'' or ''will you'' and the occasional ''please'' would be appreciated.' She shot him a severe look, at the same time loving him so fiercely that she was hard put to it not to tell him so.

He gave a crack of laughter. 'You sound just like Nanny used to! Are you going to disapprove of me for the whole trip?' He sighed over-loudly. 'And I was looking forward to a pleasant run too.'

'I have no wish to spoil your pleasure,' declared Isobel. 'How long does it last—this journey?'

'About ninety miles. We'll stop on the way for

lunch—Nanny will need a break. We'll stop in Ded-
ham at the Tolbooth and be in Orford well before tea.
I have to be back in town this evening, but half an
hour should suffice to settle you both in.'

He was working his way eastwards out of London,
going smoothly at a steady pace. 'I'll put you in the
picture as we go along,' he said presently, 'that'll save
some time when we get there.'

Isobel turned round to see if Nanny was all right.
'She's asleep,' she said, and added encouragingly:
'Yes, Dr Winter?'

'I've arranged for the bank to let you have money
if and when you need it. Mrs Cobb will see to the
shopping and so on and her husband keeps the garden
tidy. All you have to do is to keep Nanny happy and
encourage her to get out and about as much as possible. I know quite a few people there and they know
Nanny, so you'll get the occasional caller. I've arranged with Mrs Cobb to stay with Nanny for an hour
each afternoon so you can get out on your own. I
hope you won't feel tied down.'

She was surprised. 'Me? Tied down? Why should
I be? It'll be like having a summer holiday.' And
then, mindful of Bobby, 'But I would like to know
how long we're to be there, please?'

'I'll let you know that in a week's time, Isobel.'

They were clear of the suburbs now, on their way
to Chelmsford, then Colchester and a few miles further on the Tolbooth Restaurant.

Any qualms Isobel had had about getting Nanny

into the restaurant were put at rest as soon as the car was parked before its door. She might have been sure that Dr Winter, having master-minded their trip to Poland, wasn't to be deterred in such a small matter. They were expected. He carried the old lady to the powder room with Isobel in close attendance, then settled them at a corner table near the door, and all done with a minimum of fuss. Nanny, very pleased with herself in her new hat and coat, ate a good lunch and did most of the talking with an occasional encouraging word from the doctor, while Isobel sat almost silent, depressed by the thought that after today she would see almost nothing more of Thomas; they would return to London and he would go away immediately and she would never see him again. The prospect took away her appetite.

They reached Orford in mid-afternoon, looking its delightful best, with the sun shining on its charming cottages, boats moored at the quayside and the stretches of grass between the houses. They drove up Market Hill and into Pump Street and stopped before an ivy-covered brick-built house. The doctor had called it a cottage, and so had Nanny, but to Isobel's mind it was a fair-sized house, with wide sash windows and a stout white-painted front door. It was separated from the street by a narrow pavement with painted railings and tubs of geraniums on either side of the very short path, and it had an air of being lived in, which seemed surprising, since the doctor had given her to believe that it was a country retreat and nothing more.

The door opened as he got out of the car. A large, bony woman came out to meet him, then poked her head into the car to shake Nanny by the hand. 'And this'll be Nurse,' she exclaimed cheerfully. 'Come on in, I've got a kettle on the boil.'

There was a lovely tea waiting for them; scones and farm butter, cream and jam and a large fruit cake which they ate in the sitting room, a roomy apartment overlooking the street, furnished most comfortably, its open hearth ready laid with logs against the first autumn chills, still some months away. And when they had had their tea, Nanny was shown to her room just across the small square hall, and then Isobel had a look at the dining room and the kitchen with its Aga and old-fashioned wooden table and chairs and a tabby cat snoozing before the stove. It would be fun to cook on that, thought Isobel, and had her unspoken thought answered by the doctor.

'Mrs Cobb will be in each day to do the housework and washing—could you manage the cooking, Isobel?'

'Oh, yes!' She gave him a smile of pure pleasure. 'What a lovely house!'

He nodded absently; it was obvious that he was in a hurry to be gone. Indeed, Mrs Cobb had taken her upstairs, leaving him and Nanny in the sitting room, and when she got down again it was to find Nanny alone.

'Mr Thomas asked me to say goodbye—he wanted to get back.'

'Yes, of course,' said Isobel, 'he did tell me that he had to go out this evening. Nanny, I've got such a pretty room, you have no idea. I think we're going to be very comfortable here, don't you?' She made sure that the old lady was comfortable and declared her intention of unpacking for both of them and having a little talk with Mrs Cobb. The unpacking was quickly done and it took only a short time for her and Mrs Cobb to come to a comfortable understanding about housework and shopping. 'And that reminds me, Nurse,' said Mrs Cobb, 'I almost forgot, there's a wheelchair in the cupboard under the stairs—it came the other day—so that Nanny can get about a bit, I daresay. Very thoughtful of the doctor to remember.'

And very thoughtless of him not to have mentioned it to her, thought Isobel, still smarting from the manner in which he had gone off without so much as a wave of the hand.

There was plenty of food in the house. When Mrs Cobb had gone with the promise to be back at nine o'clock the next morning, Isobel cooked supper for them both, helped Nanny to bed and went upstairs to bath and get ready for her own bed, but before that she went round the rooms again. Besides the sitting room and the dining room there was a small room cosily furnished and with a small desk under the window, and beyond the kitchen there were some large

cupboards, an old-fashioned scullery where there was
a washing machine and a tumble-dryer and a door
leading into a small very pretty garden with a high
brick wall around it. There was another door too, at
the end of the hall, opposite the front door. Isobel
locked it carefully and went upstairs again. She had
been surprised to find that there were five bedrooms,
two quite small, and a splendidly appointed bathroom
as well as the shower room tucked away behind the
room Nanny was to use as a bedroom. And the rooms
were furnished with great taste and no thought of expense. She went to her own room and undressed
slowly, had a leisurely bath, then went down to see
if Nanny was already asleep. She was. Isobel left a
lamp on in the hall and the door open and started for
the stairs. She was within reach of the telephone when
it rang, and she snatched it up quickly for fear of
waking Nanny. The doctor's voice asked: 'Were you
waiting for me to ring? Such promptness!'

'Nanny has just gone to sleep and I happened to
be by the phone,' said Isobel coldly. Why should she
be civil to the wretch when he hadn't even the good
manners to say goodbye?

'Is everything all right? You have all you want?'
and when she muttered yes: 'Good. I'll leave you to
go to bed. Goodnight, Isobel.' He'd rung off before
she could say a word.

Beyond wondering wistfully what Thomas was doing, she was too tired to think much, and in the morning her common sense had returned: There was no

reason at all why he should have wished her goodbye. She was, after all, Nanny's nurse and as such had no share in his life. She got up and looked out of the window at the lovely morning and the quiet village and the sparkle of water beyond the quay, determined not to think about him.

There was plenty to fill their days. With Nanny in her wheelchair and Isobel pushing it, they explored the village street by street, went down to the quay to watch the yachts going in and out, took a look at the church of St Bartholomew and each day went back to a sparkling house, the day's shopping laid out on the kitchen table and Mrs Cobb's cheery 'Bye-bye' as she went off home for her dinner.

Nanny liked to eat in the evening and so did Isobel. She made salads and little cheesy dishes for lunch and they drank home-made lemonade before Nanny took her afternoon nap. Mrs Cobb was back by half past two and with Nanny still dozing, Isobel was free to go out if she wished to. There were a few shops where she bought their small necessities and spent pleasant minutes choosing paperbacks for Nanny, but once her small chores were done, she made her way down to the quay again and sat watching the busy scene. Each day seemed better than the last, and towards the end of the week they abandoned their afternoon walk and spent the hour before tea in the garden, Nanny with her chair shielded from the sun by an old-fashioned tussore silk parasol Isobel had unearthed from a cupboard and Isobel in a bikini, barefooted and with her hair hanging round her shoulders, lying on the grass, reading aloud.

It was Saturday and they had been there a week. Mrs Cobb had gone home and wouldn't come again until Monday and Isobel had baked a cake to have for their tea, prepared lamb cutlets for their supper, and wheeled Nanny into the shade of the plum tree in the garden. It was hot enough to lie and do nothing, but Nanny wanted to be read to. Isobel opened the book—another of the romances Nanny liked so much—and began to read.

She finished a chapter and turned the page, then glanced up to see if Nanny had gone to sleep, to find her staring at the house behind them smiling widely.

Isobel rolled over to have a look too. Standing in the open doorway were her mother and Bobby, smiling widely too. She was on her feet in a flash, hurling herself first at her mother and then her brother. 'How did you get here—how did you come? When do you...' She stopped as she caught sight of Thomas Winter coming through the hall from the open front door.

'You brought them!' she cried, and went to meet him. 'Oh, how very kind of you! I'll never be able to thank you enough. It's such a heavenly surprise to see you—all of you,' she added hastily. 'If I'd known I would have had a lovely tea waiting for you.'

He had put down the cases he was carrying and stood, very elegant in slacks and an open-necked shirt, looking down at her. He said: 'Hullo, Isobel, how well you look.' His smile made her glow all over and she remembered then that her hair was in a hopeless mess and she was in a bikini, which made her cheeks glow too.

She said shyly: 'It's too hot to take Nanny out in the afternoons, so we sit in the garden. I'll go and put on a dress.'

'Don't bother as far as I'm concerned, you'll do very nicely as you are.'

He was laughing at her now, so she said coldly: 'I'll just introduce my mother and Bobby to Nanny and go and get the tea.' And she went back into the garden, hearing him chuckle as she went.

There was no need to introduce anyone, they were already the best of friends. 'We're here for a week, darling, Thomas invited us, and he'll fetch us back next Saturday. Can you manage with the two of us extra?'

'Oh, Mother, of course! How absolutely super—I can't believe it! Look, I'm just going to get into a sundress, then we'll have tea and I'll get the rooms ready.'

'No need,' said the doctor's voice from behind her. 'I telephoned Mrs Cobb in the week and she's made up the beds and seen to the rooms.' He sauntered over to Nanny and bent to kiss her. 'Why not take your mother upstairs to her room before tea?' he suggested. 'Bobby and I will keep an eye on Nanny.' He glanced briefly at Isobel. 'I thought your mother might like the room overlooking the garden, and Bobby can have the small one next to you.'

'There's not time to talk,' said Isobel, bustling her parent upstairs. 'I must get into some clothes and get your tea—thank heavens I made a cake and some scones.'

She whisked away, tore into a sundress and sandals, brushed out her hair and raced downstairs. They were still in the garden. She went into the kitchen and began to pile cups and saucers and plates on to a tray. They could have tea out of doors, thank goodness. While she buttered scones she reorganised supper; the chops wouldn't do; she'd cook macaroni cheese and several vegetables and a fruit pie and cream. She got the cake from its tin and cut a few slices, and the doctor, who had just come in, leaned over and helped himself.

'That is nice,' he observed, studying the sundress—last year's and faded, but a pretty mixture of greens. 'The bikini was nice too.' He took a huge mouthful of cake. 'You've not lost your touch with the cooking. I expect you're working out frantic alternatives for supper tonight, but you need only cater for four, I'm going back after tea.'

He took another bite and watched through half closed eyes as telltale disappointment clouded her face. She was spooning jam from a pot into a little dish and didn't look up. 'Oh, isn't that rather a long journey all in one day? There's still a bedroom and I can cook for five just as easily as four. Besides, it is your home…'

'I'm flattered by your concern, Isobel, but it's an easy ride from here—and besides, I have to be back this evening. And now tell me, is everything going well with Nanny?'

He carried the tray out presently and they all sat about on the grass, and just for a while Isobel was completely happy. Thomas was here, sitting right beside her, and he would be back in a week's time to fetch her mother and Bobby, so she would see him again quite soon. She was a little silent savouring her happiness, but as everyone else was talking nineteen to the dozen, it wasn't noticeable, at least only to her mother's eye, and the doctor, who had his own reasons for watching her.

He went directly after tea and they all crowded to the front door to see him off, Nanny in her chair too. He kissed Nanny and Mrs Barrington, shook Bobby's hand, then came to where Isobel was standing. 'Why not?' he asked no one in particular, and kissed her too.

CHAPTER SEVEN

THE COTTAGE seemed a great deal larger once the doctor had gone, and somehow empty, but Isobel had no time to brood about that. There was Nanny to see to, supper to get, and between those a chance to talk to her mother and Bobby, although he was off in no time at all to take a look at the quay.

'So kind of Thomas,' said Mrs Barrington, 'though I can't think what put the idea into his head. He just turned up one evening and suggested it, said that you'd had no days off and this was to make up for it. Very generous of him when you think about it, inviting Bobby too.'

'What did you do with Blossom?' asked Isobel.

'That nice Cat Protection Society I sell flags for have taken her as a boarder. Thomas offered to have her at his home, but his housekeeper has got a cat and kittens and they might not have got on.'

Isobel finished laying the table and stood back to admire the effect. 'I think I'm to stay for another week or so when we get back,' she said carefully. 'Dr Winter wants to go on holiday—somewhere remote.'

Her mother followed her into the kitchen. 'Natural enough, I suppose, after all that...'

'All what?'

Her mother gave her a wide-eyed innocent look. 'Darling, if he hasn't told you, I certainly can't.'

'You seem on very friendly terms,' said Isobel tartly.

Her mother ignored the tartness. 'Oh, but we are, and he and Bobby get on very well, isn't that nice?'

Isobel opened the oven door and took a look at the macaroni cheese. 'Very,' she said.

The weather stayed warm, hot and dry, so that each day they were able to stroll down to the quay, visit the few shops or just sit in the garden. Of course Bobby spent only a little time with them; sea fishing was one of his hobbies and here he could fish from dawn to dusk, and after the first day he made friends with one or two of the boat owners and went off with them, down to the Ness and out to sea, coming back with fish for the next day's dinner. And extra company certainly did Nanny good. She and Mrs Barrington sat happily discussing everything under the sun while Isobel gave Mrs Cobb a hand round the house or got the meals. There was really nothing to do for Nanny now; she was walking just a little with the aid of a stick and provided there was someone to help her round the house when they got back, Isobel could see no reason why she should stay. It would be better, she decided, if she were to go as soon as possible now—get a job, if possible, miles away where there was no chance of seeing Thomas ever again or being anywhere where she might be reminded of him.

Perhaps there would be a chance to tell him so when he came at the weekend.

It was a long week despite her well filled days, but Saturday came at last with a message at breakfast time that the doctor would be with them for lunch. Bobby had answered the phone, and when his mother asked if he had been told if they were going back that day or not, he looked vague and said that he hadn't thought of asking.

'Boys!' sighed Mrs Barrington resignedly, and went back to pack their cases. 'Because I'm sure Thomas will want to get back so that he can spend Sunday with all those friends of his.'

But that was no reason why they shouldn't have a splendid lunch, a kind of culinary farewell, Isobel decided. She popped out to the shops and came back with fresh salmon and a few extra ingredients to augment the salad. It would have to be an apricot flan for pudding; there had been fresh apricots at the greengrocers, and she had bought extra cream; she could make the pastry while the salmon mousse was setting. Bobby had already seen to the potatoes before he had escaped to the quay and she had all the morning.

Her mother and Nanny were in the garden and Mrs Cobb was upstairs making beds. Isobel shut herself in the kitchen and got to work.

The mousse was setting nicely, the salad was made and the potatoes were in their saucepan and the ladies had had their coffee. Isobel was arranging apricots in the flan case when the kitchen door opened behind her.

'There's nothing for you to eat,' she said, not bothering to turn round. 'If you're as famished as all that you'll find biscuits in the tin in the cupboard.' She added, wheedling: 'Bobby, be a darling and put those two bottles of white wine in the fridge, before you get at those biscuits.'

'I'll be a darling and uncork the wine,' said the doctor from the kitchen door, 'but I haven't come all this way just to eat biscuits.'

She spun round to look at him. 'Oh!' she said breathlessly. 'You're early.'

'A cold welcome and dry biscuits,' said the doctor. 'For two pins I won't see to the wine.'

'Oh, I'm sorry—I thought you were Bobby and I didn't think you'd get here for another hour and I was going to have everything quite ready for you. I expect you want to get back again as soon as possible.' Isobel arranged the last of the fruit and popped the flan into the oven. 'Mother has packed.'

'Glad to be going?' he asked blandly.

'Of course not—they've loved every single minute.'

'I'm glad to hear it. I planned to stay until tomorrow tea time—if that's not too late for your mother and Bobby.'

'Oh, no, they'll be glad.' She beamed at him, so happy that she forgot to hide her feelings. 'Mother's in the garden and Bobby's down at the quay—he's made so many friends…if you like to go into the garden I'll bring you some coffee and a slice of cake.'

'I'll have it here. I like watching you cook. A woman's place is in the home, so I've been told, though I can't call to mind many young women who do that these days.'

He came and sat on the table and ate the best part of the cake she had made for tea; luckily she had made a second one, thinking it would keep nicely for later in the week. He drank all the coffee there was in the pot, too, and then with a careless remark that he would take his case up to his room, he strolled away. Isobel heard him then in the garden, and when she peeped out, he was lying stretched out at the ladies' feet, presumably asleep. She put the finishing touches to the salad, laid another place at the table and ran upstairs to tidy herself. She uttered a moan of horror when she saw herself in the mirror; hair all over the place, no make-up left after all that cooking in the warm kitchen, and an elderly cotton dress she wore only for cooking and housework.

She changed into the blue cotton dress, the one she had worn the first time she had seen Thomas, did her hair with great neatness and made up her face as best she could; she was so brown now that her powder didn't match, so she applied lipstick and left her face to shine.

The doctor had taken drinks out into the garden, sherry for Nanny and Mrs Barrington, a soft drink for Bobby, who had just turned up, and beer for himself, and when Isobel joined them, 'I'm not going to ask you what you want,' he told her. 'I got you a Dubonnet with lots of ice and lemon.'

It sounded somehow as though they had had drinks together so often that he knew exactly what she liked. She thanked him composedly and sat down, avoiding her mother's thoughtful eye.

Lunch went down well, and afterwards the doctor and Bobby washed up and the went off to fish, which gave Isobel the chance to make another cake, cut a plateful of sandwiches, settle Nanny for a nap and then sit in the garden with her mother.

'I suppose you'll be back next weekend?' her mother asked casually.

'I think so. Dr Winter's going away as soon as we get back, isn't he? Now Nanny's so much better I should be able to get home for an afternoon now and again.'

'That'll be nice, dear. Let's hope that the next case is as interesting as this one.'

Isobel didn't look at her mother. 'Yes, I thought I'd get right away if there's anything going—out of London.'

'What a good idea,' agreed her parent cheerfully. 'Do you want any help with supper, darling?'

'No, thanks—luckily there were half a dozen lamb cutlets in the freezer, peas and broad beans and mint sauce, and there are some prawns. I'll make prawn cocktails for starters and fresh fruit salad and cream for dessert. Will that do?'

'Admirably. What a blessing that you can cook, dear. We aren't going until after lunch tomorrow, are we?'

'No, but I'd planned roast pork anyway. We shall eat it all at one go, but I can get something else for the two of us in the week. And I'll make a trifle later on.'

'We do keep you busy, but it's nice that Thomas enjoys his food. Has he got a good cook?'

'Mrs Gibson the housekeeper cooks; she's super too.'

'A well run household, I've no doubt,' observed Mrs Barrington.

The men came back presently with a dozen mackerel which they insisted on cleaning before tea, sternly advised by Isobel to leave the kitchen spotless when they had finished. 'Tartar!' said Thomas, grinning at her. 'You're as bad as a nagging wife!'

Only if I were your wife, I wouldn't nag you, promised Isobel silently.

The weekend went too fast. In no time at all Isobel was standing at the door of the cottage with Nanny standing bravely beside her, leaning on her stick, waving them all goodbye. The doctor was coming to fetch them during the week, probably at tea time, and she had been told to be ready to leave on Wednesday unless he telephoned otherwise. He had told her quite casually just before they left and all she could say was: 'Very well, we'll be waiting for you. Shall I tell Mrs Cobb and pay any bills?'

For some reason he had smiled then. 'Yes, do that. How indispensable you've made yourself, Isobel—I don't know what we're going to do without you.'

She hadn't answered him because she couldn't think of what to say. Something lighthearted if only she could have thought of it, instead of wanting to burst into tears. He had turned away to kiss Nanny and then waved a careless hand at her as he got into the car. She had ignored all that and made some bright remark to her mother, sitting in splendour on the back seat. Nanny had waved, but Isobel's hands felt glued to her sides.

The doctor returned on Wednesday, just as he had said he would, at tea time. Isobel and Nanny were both ready to leave, so it was just a question of putting the kettle on and fetching down their bags. Mrs Cobb had been bidden goodbye with the promise of instructions from Dr Winter at a later date, small bills had been paid and meticulously accounted for by Isobel, together with the remainder of the money she had had for housekeeping expenses. There was nothing left to do but to greet him politely when he arrived and give him his tea.

Isobel, now that it was time to go, didn't want to leave. The cottage had begun to seem like home and she had made a few friends here and there and there had been time to dream a little; impossible dreams, of course, but very comforting. Nanny was sorry to be leaving too, but not too much so. Once back in London she would have her niece and her family to

visit and Mrs Gibson with whom to gossip. She plied
the doctor with questions over tea and he answered
her patiently. He looked tired, Isobel thought, and a
holiday would do him the world of good. She wondered if Ella would be going with him, or if not Ella,
someone else. She wished for the hundredth time that
she knew more about him.

She cleared away presently and washed up the tea
things and left everything tidy: Mrs Cobb would be
in the following morning to put the place to rights,
but Isobel whisked round the cottage making sure that
everything was just so while Nanny was being got
into the car, and then got in herself and waited while
Thomas locked the door. They drove back to London
very fast and none of them had much to say. Nanny
was tired by the time they arrived back and Isobel,
accompanied by a solicitous Mrs Gibson, bore her off
to bed, stood over her while she ate the delicious supper prepared for her and then went to her room to
unpack her bag and tidy herself. Not quite sure what
was expected of her, she went downstairs presently,
to be met by Gibson in the hall.

'Dinner's ready for you in the dining room, Nurse,'
he informed her, 'and Dr Winter wished me to say
that he will see you in the morning.'

A not very satisfactory ending to their return.

Nanny was up and dressed and sipping her mid-
morning coffee by the time Isobel was sent for by the
doctor. He had gone out very early, Gibson had told
her—some emergency at the hospital, and now he had

come back briefly before going to his rooms to see his morning patients.

So he would be tired and possibly ill-tempered as well as hungry. Isobel crossed the hall and went into his study.

If he was any of these things, he didn't show it. He was as immaculate as he always was, his face bland, a tray of coffee at his elbow. His good morning was pleasant as he waved her to a chair. 'I'm sorry we've had no opportunity to talk—I've got about five minutes to spare now, though. I'd be glad if you'd stay until Sunday, Isobel. I shall be leaving quite early in the morning, so you'll be free to go as soon as you wish after that. Nanny has made a splendid recovery and Mrs Gibson feels she'll be able to manage with some extra daily help. I'll let the agency know, and leave a cheque for you…'

'The agency usually…' began Isobel.

'Yes, but I prefer to pay you myself, just as I did the first time. It only remains for me to thank you once more. Nanny and I are most grateful to you for all you've done.'

He was a stranger, polite and distant and withdrawn. Isobel stood up. 'Nanny has been a wonderful patient. I hope you'll have a very good holiday, Dr Winter. Shall I see you again before you leave?'

'Well, I shall be out this evening and I have guests coming to dinner on Saturday, but I daresay we'll have the chance to say goodbye before Sunday.' And as she went to the door, 'Take the car if you want to run Nanny over to see her niece.'

Isobel said thank you in her quiet voice and closed the door silently behind her. It seemed likely that whatever he said she wasn't going to see him again. She wouldn't allow herself to think about it, but went back to Nanny and began at once to embark on plans to drive over to Peckham.

But she did see him once more, on the following evening, coming up the stairs two at a time towards her as she was on her way down to get Nanny's supper tray. She summoned a normal voice and wished him a good evening, and was surprised when he stopped beside her. 'There's something I've been meaning to ask you. Why don't you want me to see that you wear the amber necklace? You wear it—I've seen it under your dress.'

He put out a hand and gently tapped its slight bulge.

Isobel looked round for inspiration and found none. After a minute she said: 'It reminds me of Poland.' She blushed as she said it and then stared at him surprised when he said with a kind of angry impatience:

'I need nothing to remind me of Poland—or, for that matter, of you.'

He bent his head suddenly and kissed her hard, then went on upstairs without another word. She didn't see him before she left. People came to the house that evening, she could hear them from her room where she had asked, very firmly, if she might have her dinner. The doctor had been angry when she had refused to join him and his guests at table; if he hadn't been so coldly annoyed she would have explained that she had nothing suitable to wear, that she knew none of his friends, that she would feel like a fish out of water. As it was, she gave no explanation at all, and he had agreed in a tight-lipped fashion. She thought of that as she ate her solitary meal and listened to the muted sounds of people enjoying themselves downstairs.

She took care not to go down in the morning until she heard the unmistakable sounds of his departure, and since saying goodbye was a painful business, she made as short work as possible of her goodbyes, and with the cautious promise that provided she wasn't working, she would come and see Nanny whenever she could, she got into the car beside Gibson and was driven home.

The little house looked closed and forlorn as Gibson pulled up in front of it, and Isobel could see Blossom peering through the sitting room window, looking disconsolate. Gibson put down her case at the door and she urged him not to wait. 'My mother's out, I expect,' she told him. 'Besides, it's your day off and I've taken up too much of your time already.' She shook his hand and thanked him and watched him drive away before opening the door, setting her case in the hall and going into the sitting room.

Blossom came rushing at her, mewing unhappily, and Isobel picked her up and carried her through to the kitchen and fed her, then she opened the back door so that she could go into the garden. Her mother must have gone out unexpectedly, as although she hadn't known exactly when Isobel was coming home, she had known it would be Sunday; besides, she didn't go out on Sunday except to church, and it was too early for that.

She lugged her case upstairs, put it in her room and then, not knowing quite why she did it, pushed open the door of her mother's bedroom on the other side of the tiny landing. Mrs Barrington was lying on the floor by the bed. She was in her nightdress and dressing gown and there was a broken cup and saucer and a still damp patch of tea on the floor beside her.

Isobel's heart seemed to stop for a moment, then she knelt down and took her mother's pulse; faint but fairly steady. It was obvious that her mother was unconscious and she could see no sign of injury. She put a pillow under her head, covered her with her quilt from the bed and flew to the phone.

Her mother's doctor was away for the weekend, and his stand-in was out on a case. Isobel left an urgent message, wishing with all her heart that Thomas had been somewhere where she could have got hold of him. That he would have come at once she never doubted, but wishing the impossible wasn't going to help matters; she went back to her mother and began to examine her methodically, just as though she were a patient brought into Casualty. Her pulse was stronger and there was a tinge of colour in her face, although she made no response to Isobel's voice or touch.

'CVA,' said Isobel out loud. 'Not too bad, thank God, at least I think so. I wish that doctor would come…'

She heard the car draw up as she said it and went to let him in. He was a stranger, a small mild man who introduced himself as Dr Watts and wasted no time in small talk. Nor did Isobel; she took about two minutes to lay the facts before him and then led him upstairs.

She had been right. Her mother had had a stroke—not, thank heaven, a serious one. They got her back into bed and when he suggested that she should go to hospital, Isobel heard the reluctance in his voice.

'I'm a trained nurse, between cases,' she told him. 'I can nurse Mother here just as well as if she went to hospital—probably better, because it's only a question of care and feeding and patience, isn't it? Is it a thrombosis or haemorrhage, do you think?'

'I'm not sure at this stage. As soon as your mother regains consciousness we shall be able to see if she has any paralysis. I'll telephone Dr Martin in the morning, but I'll be round again this evening to see how she is.' He looked at Isobel anxiously. 'You're sure you can manage?'

'Quite sure, Doctor.'

And manage she did, through the first few anxious days when her mother became conscious again, and although unable to speak clearly and use her right arm

and leg, demonstrated quite clearly that she was going
to get better. Then there were the long tedious days
of feeding and nursing and getting in and out of bed
to sit in a chair by the window, the careful exercises,
the doctor's visits and above all the constantly cheerful face and voice.

Isobel never faltered, at least not in front of her
mother or Dr Martin, and at night she was so tired
that she couldn't put two thoughts together before she
was almost asleep. But those two thoughts were always the same—a longing for Thomas and sheer ter-
ror as to the future. She wasn't earning; her mother's
small pension was just enough to pay the rent and
maintenance of the little house once the food was paid
for; her earnings had covered Bobby's fees, his
clothes and their meagre comforts. Now she was dig-
ging into the money put aside for those, and the night-
mare of not having the school fees for the next term
was something she went to bed with every night.

That it was silly to wish for Thomas was something
she acknowledged; it was like wanting the moon or
the stars. After the first week or so she managed to
douse the very thought of him. She had found time
to write to Nanny, making light of her mother's illness but making it the reason for her not visiting the
old lady, and she had a letter back almost at once,
full of little titbits of news, although the doctor wasn't
mentioned. Quite clearly Nanny had no inkling of the
severity of Mrs Barrington's illness, for she wrote
quite cheerfully that Isobel must be looking forward

to another case. 'And mind you come and see us all when you have the time,' the letter ended.

Mrs Barrington was as mettlesome as her daughter. Not for one moment did she allow herself to despair; the only thing which worried her was the fact that Isobel was tied to the house, day in, day out. True, she tore out to the local shops once or twice a week and spent an hour in the garden every afternoon, while her mother had her rest, playing with Blossom and pottering among the roses, cutting the tiny lawn and trimming the hedge. None of the neighbours had called, but she hadn't expected them to. London, she had learned a long while ago, could be a lonely place. In the village where she had lived everyone knew everyone else, at least by sight, and to pass anyone without a greeting was unheard-of, and as for being ill, neighbours would be round within the hour with offers of help. During her brief spells of doing nothing Isobel began to think seriously of ways and means of getting out of London. It would be difficult, probably impossible, but there might be a way...

In the meantime she pressed on with the task of getting her mother back to her usual self once more. A masseuse came twice a week and on the other days Isobel contrived to be her substitute, and now that her mother was sitting for a good deal of the day in a chair, she was going to do more and more for herself. All the same, progress was slow even if steady, and Isobel, worried sick about the lack of money and how she was going to manage during the next few months until her mother was on her feet again, got thin and pale, and her looks, never remarkable, suffered. Only her eyes kept their deep blue, looking much too large in her peaky face. Dr Martin came twice a week now, declaring himself well satisfied with his patient's progress, urging Isobel to take more exercise. 'Get someone in to sit with your mother,' he suggested. 'I'd send the practice nurse, only she's up to her eyes with this whooping cough epidemic.' He hurried to the door, a busy man. 'I'll be in at the end of the week—let's see, it's just over three weeks, isn't it? Your mother has done very well—she's a wonderful woman, and you are a splendid nurse. You must turn a room downstairs into a bedroom, Isobel, so that your mother can try to get around the house. She's doing well with the zimmer.'

To all of which Isobel cheerfully agreed, and once he had gone, sat down to ponder the problem of getting a bed downstairs into the poky little dining room, rearranging the furniture and conveying her mother downstairs. As for the holiday, she didn't dare think of that.

She was up early next morning, tidying the house, seeing to her mother, getting breakfast. Dr Martin wouldn't be coming for two days, which gave her time to get her mother downstairs. She knew exactly what she had to do, and once her mother was settled in her chair, the bell by her good hand, her book propped up so that she could read, Isobel went into the dining room. Luckily there wasn't a great deal of furniture in it; a rather nice gate-leg table, four chairs and a graceful mahogany sideboard. The sideboard would have to stay, the table and chairs must somehow be fitted into the sitting room. She had decided to bring her own small bed downstairs; it was easier to move than Bobby's, and she could sleep there while he was away at school. The thought reminded her that in about ten weeks' time his fees would be due and she had already dipped into her savings. She brushed it aside; first things first.

She had heaved the table into the hall, lifted the chairs on top of it and squeezed her way round them to get back into the dining room, when the front door bell rang. It wasn't the day to pay the milkman or the baker, it could be the man for the rent, a day early. Isobel squeezed her way back again and opened the door.

Dr Winter stood on the doorstep, filling the entire doorway. She goggled up at him, the instant delight which filled her considerably damped down by the thought that she wasn't dressed for the occasion. An elderly cotton dress, a plastic pinny with 'All hands on deck' printed across its front, her hair, not at its best, tied back anyhow with a bit of ribbon. She opened her mouth closed it and then opened it again to utter: 'Oh, dear!'

But Thomas had seen the delight, although he gave no sign, only sighed inwardly. Here was a situation which would need instant and careful handling.

His 'good morning' was pleasantly bland, and since

she had no choice but to invite him Isobel bade him enter. A difficult business, she realised, too late. The table and chairs, and the doctor with her squashed in between them, made an awkward situation. She stayed where she was and waited for him to speak.

'I've come to see your mother—I've had a chat with Dr Martin and he has no objection. Perhaps there's something I can do...I'm very sorry to hear that she's been ill, but he tells me she's making a wonderful recovery.' His keen eyes took in her neglected hair and shining nose and the dreadful pinny. 'Due largely to your nursing, I'm told.'

She didn't answer; for one thing she was so happy despite her untidy person, that she had lost her voice. Miracles happened, after all; for what other reason could there be for Thomas to come out of the blue like this when she had imagined him to be in some exotic place miles away?

'If I might see her?' prompted the doctor gently. 'Are you spring-cleaning?'

Isobel found her voice. 'No, just getting the room ready for Mother—Dr Martin thought it would be a good thing to get her downstairs now that she's well—well, not quite walking, but on her feet, at any rate.' She squeezed past him. 'If you could manage past the table.'

It was a silly thing to say, his massive bulk couldn't possibly get through such a small space. He lifted the chairs down and moved the table back into the dining room and professed himself ready to follow her upstairs.

He had, Isobel had to admit, a splendid bedside manner. He greeted Mrs Barrington like an old friend, shook her hand, professed himself delighted to see how well she was recovering and then suggested that, since Dr Martin had no objection, he might be allowed to examine her. Then he listened without a trace of impatience while Mrs Barrington explained how she had become ill and how frightened she had been and how determined to get well again. She still spoke slowly with slightly slurred speech, but her eyes were alive and alert. She owed her recovery to Isobel, she told him. 'More than three weeks, and the child has hardly been outside the door, and no help either.'

The doctor nodded sympathetically. 'Well, let's get you on the bed and take a look, shall we?'

He took a long time, with Isobel, having shed the pinny, once more a nurse. 'You know, you're almost there, Mrs Barrington. A few weeks' intense physiotherapy and some speech therapy and you'll be as good as new. I have beds in a small private hospital near my home, I want you to go there for a little while. Would you agree if I arrange it?'

He was looking at her and smiling, although he shot a lightning glance at Isobel, whose face betrayed her thoughts only too plainly; he sighed again behind imperturbable features. 'You must be tired now—suppose you have a short nap on your bed while Isobel and I get the matter settled?'

Isobel tucked her mother under the eiderdown and led the way downstairs to the sitting room. She offered him a shabby but elegant wingback chair and shut the door behind her.

'Well, Isobel?' asked the doctor without waste of time.

She sat down rather primly in a small balloon-backed chair facing him.

'I don't understand,' she said in a voice which shook a little despite her calm face. 'How did you find out about Mother's illness? And why did you come here? And before we settle anything, there's one thing you must understand. I'm deeply grateful for your offer to take Mother into your hospital—and why you had to say so, I can't think—but it's quite impossible. I'm not working for the moment, my mother's pension is small and she has no capital. There are Bobby's school fees to consider...'

'I take it that you pay those?' interpolated the doctor quietly.

'Well, yes, I do, but the thing is I've had to take some of the money to—to buy one or two things Mother had to have...' She paused. 'And there's no one I can borrow money from to pay for her fees, you must understand that—we haven't any family, no one at all, just the three of us.' She sounded suddenly fierce. 'And up until now we've managed very well and shall again. I know it will take longer for Mother to get well, but when the masseuse came the first time she showed me what to do, and I can help her walk…'

The doctor sat back in his chair and stretched out his long legs with the air of a man who had all the time in the world. 'Isobel, have you looked at yourself lately?' And when she didn't answer: 'Before your mother is fully recovered you'll be flat on your face. You're too thin, you're tired to death, probably you don't eat enough or take much exercise. Oh, I know you are on your feet all day, but that's not the same thing. And I wasn't aware that the question of fees had arisen. I consider your mother to be a friend, and as such she will be treated without any charges.'

'You're very kind,' said Isobel stiffly, 'but I won't accept charity…'

'No? You would allow your mother to remain just a little slow in her speech, just a little paralysed, just to be a little bit tired for the rest of her life so that you may justify a pig-headed pride? I'm disappointed in you, Isobel.'

She looked down at her hands, folded neatly on her lap, and could scarcely see them for tears. 'But I haven't any money,' she muttered. 'You must try and understand—we rent this house, the furniture's nice, but it wouldn't fetch enough—besides, Mother must have a home and these things are all she has left. Even if I asked you to lend me the money, I wouldn't be able to pay you back for years…'

'It's very simple, Isobel.' His voice was quiet,

placid even. 'Your pride against your mother's recovery. And what is money compared with good health and life? Your mother's health, Isobel.' His voice was suddenly harsh. 'And I wasn't aware that I'd asked any fees.'

She still didn't look up. 'Could you really get her quite well again?'

'Yes.'

'And would you keep an account of—of what it will cost so that I can repay you when I can?'

The doctor examined his carefully trimmed nails. 'Certainly I will.' He added casually: 'Have you made serious inroads into Bobby's school fees?'

She forgot for the moment that she had no intention of telling him about her difficulties. 'Yes, but if I can go back to work soon I can pay it back. I can earn a lot more if I do night duty or go without my days off or look after a mental patient.'

'Just at the moment you aren't fit to look after anyone, not even yourself, Isobel.'

She looked up then, her eyes wide with apprehension, but before she could utter, he went on: 'I'll make arrangements for your mother to go to the hospital—' he mentioned a clinic by name— 'this afternoon.' He frowned. 'Surely there's someone you can go and stay with for a few days?'

She shook her head. 'Besides, there's Blossom.'

'You will come back with me, Isobel, and Blossom shall come with you, and you'll do nothing at all for at least two days. After that you can find yourself another case.' He looked around the little room. 'You can't stay here alone.'

'Oh, but I...'

'I must ask you not to argue, Isobel. I got back from the Caribbean this morning early and I have a touch of jet lag. Now go and pack a few things for your mother and be ready to leave here in an hour's time.'

She said fiercely, 'Yes, but that's all very well—how did you know...?'

'I have ways of finding out. Now be a good girl and do as I ask.' He stood up, towering above her head, and she got up too. She said with belated politeness, 'I hope you had a good holiday.'

He was at the door but he turned round to answer her. 'I've just spent two weeks with Ella,' he said.

It was silly to cry, she dried her eyes and went upstairs and began to pack a bag for her mother, embarking on a cheerful conversation about a rosy future, which, however much it cheered Mrs Barrington, held no comfort for her.

The doctor was as good as his word. Precisely on the hour the Rolls drew up before the front door. He got out and rang the bell, not noticing the twitching lace curtains in the houses on either side of him, and when Isobel opened the door he wasted no time, but lifted her mother into the car, put the luggage in the boot, Blossom in her basket on the back seat, shut the front door briskly and urged Isobel to get in beside him. He had barely spoken, and Isobel was glad of that; her head was full of the small problems of their sudden departure. Had she given the milkman sufficient warning? Had she double locked the back door? She had turned off the electricity; should she have done the same for the water? She had turned off the gas too, and taken everything perishable—and that wasn't much—round to the surly woman who lived next door. She had phoned the landlord and promised to send on the rent. She closed her eyes for a moment and didn't see the doctor's sharp glance. She had changed into her blue dress and done her hair and looked as neat as she usually did, only she was a bit too thin and pale.

And that was the opinion Mrs Gibson was quick to offer when she saw her. 'You're to come right upstairs with me, Nurse, doctor's orders, and go to bed. I'll bring you a nice lunch, presently. You shall see Nanny later, he says, but first you're to sleep.'

Isobel, in the room she had had previously, felt like bursting into tears again. 'Oh, please, Mrs Gibson, may I have a bath first? I'll be quick...'

So she had a bath and washed her hair, then got into bed and ate the delicious lunch Mrs Gibson brought up, and when the tray had been taken away she lay back on her pillows, thinking about the day's happenings.

Her mother wasn't far away. The clinic was a fairly small one in an elegant street not five minutes' walk from Thomas's house. She had been taken to a charming room on the ground floor and the Matron had listened to the doctor with the air of someone who wouldn't wish to vex him in any way, and Isobel, standing in the background, couldn't help but see that his air of authority carried a good deal of weight. She had bidden her mother goodbye and felt reassured to see her parent remarkably cheerful and happy. 'And you'll have a few days' rest, darling,' her mother had said, 'and you deserve every minute of them.'

And now here she was, tucked up in her bed in this delightful room with Blossom asleep on her feet, and she really must set her mind to making some sort of plan for the future. She closed her eyes the better to think, and was sleeping in the instant. The doctor, coming up to visit her, stood in the doorway, smiling a little. Lying in bed with her hair loose around her sleeping face, her gentle mouth slightly open, she looked surprisingly pretty.

CHAPTER EIGHT

ISOBEL WAS SITTING UP in bed eating an enormous breakfast when Thomas knocked and walked in. His 'good morning' was as impersonal as a family doctor's and his glance even more so. 'Slept well?' he wanted to know. 'Get up if you feel like it, if you don't stay in bed, but be in bed by nine o'clock.'

'When can I see Mother?' She had a slice of toast, laden with butter and marmalade in her hand, ready to bite into.

'Not today.' He gave her a reassuring smile. 'I'll be seeing her later on, I'll let you know how she is. Tomorrow, if you feel really rested, there's no reason why you shouldn't see her.'

'It's very kind of you to have me here, but I'll go home after I've seen Mother, if you don't mind. I can get a case straight away, somewhere where I can go home each evening—because of Blossom, you know.'

He gave her a hard look. 'Just as you like, Isobel. But I beg you to allow your mother to stay where she is until her cure is complete. Are you all right for money?'

Isobel went a slow red. 'I can fetch Mother's pension at the end of the week.'

He nodded. 'I must be off, I've got a full day.

Please remember what I've said. Mrs Gibson will get you anything you want.'

Everything but you, dear Thomas, thought Isobel, watching him go.

She got up presently and went along to see Nanny, now in a room of her own downstairs. They had coffee together and then Isobel went to the kitchen to talk to Gibson and his wife, a placid Blossom draped over one shoulder. She had her lunch with Nanny and after lunch, just as she was being urged to go and rest on her bed until tea time, the doctor rang.

'Your mother is fine,' he told her without preamble. 'She's had her therapy and settled in nicely. She sends her love. I hope you're doing exactly as I said?'

'Yes, Dr Winter, and thank you for letting me know about Mother.'

'Will you be good enough to tell Gibson I shan't be home for dinner?' His 'goodbye' was brisk and he hung up at once.

Obediently Isobel went to bed at nine o'clock after a leisurely session at the dressing table. A good sleep and a lazy day had worked wonders, but she longed for a row of expensive creams and lotions to turn her into instant prettiness. As it was, she slapped on most of a pot of night cream someone had given her for Christmas, brushed her hair, and got into her bed, where she sat doing terrifying sums in the notebook she always carried with her. The fees at the nursing home would be astronomical, not to mention speech therapy and physio, and she was determined to pay back every penny. If she got a job right away—night duty for preference—and she was very careful, her mother's pension would be untouched and could be saved together with most of her earnings. All the same, at a rough guess, it was going to take years to pay back the doctor. The slow tears dripped down her cheeks and she didn't bother to wipe them away, there were plenty more ready to follow them. She put the notebook down and closed her eyes.

The doctor, coming in at one o'clock in the morning, paused in the corridor when he saw the light under her door, and when no one answered his knock, he went in. He stood for quite some time in the open doorway, looking at Isobel, fast asleep, her face shiny with cream, runnelled by tear stains, her hair tousled. Blossom was curled up on her feet and the notebook lay where she had put it down. The doctor crossed the room soundlessly and picked it up and studied it at his leisure, his face expressionless, then he put it back again, tickled Blossom's matronly chin, and went away. It was difficult to find a greater contrast between two girls—the lovely spoilt expensive young woman he had spent the evening with, and Isobel's unremarkable, shiny visage, and yet it was her face which was uppermost in his mind; had been for some time now, he had to admit. He went downstairs again, and into his study, to bury his handsome head in a pile of medical journals; reading them might clear his head of the ridiculous ideas invading it.

Isobel got up as soon as she had had breakfast, which Mrs Gibson had insisted on bringing her in bed. 'And I'm to tell you from the doctor that he has to be away until late this evening, but that you're to visit your mother when you wish and you're to ask Gibson to drive you back home. He said to tell you he's sure that you'll get another case very quickly and you're to get in touch with him if the need arises. Oh, and I almost forgot, Dr Martin—is that the name?— will let you know how your mother is progressing. There, I think I've remembered everything.' She beamed at Isobel. 'Now you eat your breakfast—and why don't you stay another day or two? Nanny loves to have you here, and you're not a scrap of trouble.'

Isobel summoned a smile. 'You're all so kind, Mrs Gibson, but I really must get back to work. I've had a really good rest and I feel as fit as a prize-fighter. I'll go and see Mother—and may I leave Blossom with Nanny while I'm gone? I'll be back before lunch and perhaps Gibson would be kind enough to take me home then?'

'You'll have your lunch here, Nurse dear, and no nonsense, and Gibson shall take you home when you've eaten it.'

Isobel was dressed and sitting at the pretty dressing table doing the best she could with her face when there was a knock on the door. Mrs Gibson with coffee, she had no doubt, or a message from Nanny to have it with her. It was neither. It was Ella Stokes, stunning in a suede skirt and a sheer silk blouse with nothing but flesh beneath it. Her hair was tossed into a carefully untidy mop and she had one of those shoulder bags which cost the earth slung over one shoulder. Isobel, eyeing all this, was struck dumb with surprise and envy, but before she could find her tongue, Ella spoke.

'Hullo,' she said, and smiled widely. 'I say, I came to say how sorry I was to hear about your mother—what rotten luck for her, and for you; you can't work, of course. She's getting better, though, isn't she? Trust Thomas for that; he enjoys pulling people back from the brink—oh, sorry, I shouldn't have said that—and he's so stinking rich that he'll not even notice the expense. You won't need to pay him back. Besides, I put in a good word for you and said you'd never be able to afford to, and he owes you a good turn after all you've done for Nanny.'

She sat down on the bed and Isobel said in a colourless voice, 'That was kind of you, but I don't need any help, thank you, and I prefer to manage my own affairs. The doctor knows that.'

Ella's tinkly laugh rang out. 'Oh, I know that too—what was it he called you? Prickly—he meant it nicely, of course.'

'Of course,' Isobel agreed gently. 'Why have you come here to see me?'

Ella's eyes widened. 'Why, to say how sorry I am, of course.' She got up and strolled to the door. 'I told Thomas I'd come; he's so good to the people who work for him, and I intend to be the same. Goodbye, Isobel.'

Isobel stared at her reflection in the triple mirror; it stared back at her, pale with rage and misery. She supposed that it was natural enough for a man to confide in the girl he was going to marry, and she had no right to mind that, but he need not have called her prickly or discussed her finances... Once again she sought fruitlessly for some means whereby she could pay the hospital fees. There were none.

She packed everything, so that she would be able to leave as soon as she had had lunch, took Blossom down to Nanny's room, and walked round to the clinic.

Her mother was up and dressed, walking up and down the corridor outside her room, a stick in one hand, the physiotherapist beside her. She was delighted to see Isobel and full of praise for the clinic. 'I'll be home in no time at all,' she told Isobel in her slurred voice. 'They're so kind and helpful and I know I'm going to get quite better. And you look rested, darling. Are you going home soon?'

'Today, Mother. I'll try and get a case not too far away and I'll let you know as soon as I'm settled with one. I'll take Blossom with me and only go somewhere where I can come home each day.'

'Dear Thomas,' said Mrs Barrington, 'how kind he's been! He came to see me yesterday and he's coming again this evening. He says I've responded so well that it will only be two or three weeks. I'm so grateful, and to you, darling, for all you've done for me.' The physiotherapist had walked a little apart. 'We are all right for money, aren't we?'

'Yes, Mother,' said Isobel steadily. 'There's nothing to worry about at all, all you have to do is get quite well.' She kissed her mother's cheek. 'Goodbye, love, I'll be along to see you as soon as I can, and I'll telephone tomorrow.'

At least her mother was going to be all right, she reflected as she walked back to the doctor's house, and that was all that mattered.

Home looked small and shabby and unwelcoming. Gibson had put her case in the hall for her, bade her a goodbye in a voice which held regret—the same regret Mrs Gibson and Nanny had shown. She had left a polite note for the doctor, a bread-and-butter letter which betrayed none of her true feelings, and now here she was, back in the little terraced house once more. She let Blossom into the back garden, put on a load of washing and made a pot of tea and presently telephoned the agency.

The agency lady was inclined to be huffy. Isobel had been one of the most reliable members, ready to take on anything at a moment's notice, and sick mother or no, she had been away all of three weeks. But the urgency in Isobel's voice melted the huffiness a little. She said severely: 'If you'll wait a moment I will see what I have in my files. You say it must be night duty and living out?'

She had exactly the right case on her files; she had already offered it to two other nurses who had refused it, but she had no intention of letting Isobel know that. 'It just so happens,' she said with the right amount of hesitancy, 'that there is a case—came in this morning.' She added mendaciously: 'Night duty, seven nights a week and live out. An elderly widow recovering from pneumonia and suffering from insomnia.

She dislikes sleeping tablets and although she has living-in staff, she doesn't want their night's rest disturbed.' She added to clinch the matter: 'The pay is good; night duty seven nights a week—I know it's not acceptable, but it should be a short case.'

Isobel was doing sums on the back of an envelope. The money would be beyond her wildest dreams, and it really didn't matter what kind of patient she had, the thing was to get back on to a financial even keel once more.

'I'll take it,' she said. 'And am I wanted tonight?'

The agency lady heaved a sigh of relief that Isobel didn't hear. 'If possible. Here's the address, very handy for you.' She read out a house number and a street in Chelsea, very near the Embankment. 'You can get a bus across Battersea Bridge. The hours are half past eight until half past eight with half an hour for a meal during the night.' She added cautiously: 'There's no mention of breakfast, but I should suppose they would give you something before you leave each morning.'

It was nice to have something to do; it took her mind off Thomas and her mother. She hung out the washing, made up the bed, nipped smartly to the local shops and stocked up food for herself and Blossom, then returned to attend to the little cat's needs, cook a quick meal for herself and change into uniform. With Blossom safely in her basket, the doors and windows securely shut and the washing brought in, Isobel left the house. She had allowed herself time enough to reach the destination, but it was important to get there punctually on her first evening; she might have to wait for a bus, or not find the street at once.

As it turned out, a bus came along just as she reached the bus stop and she found the street without any difficulty. The house was half way down a terrace of Edwardian red brick houses, substantial, ugly and much sought after. Isobel turned on her heel with a good fifteen minutes to spare and walked back to the Embankment, to present herself, exactly on time, when those minutes were up.

A neat maid opened the door, wearing, most unusually, a black dress and a white apron and cap. She looked pleased to see Isobel and ushered her into a small room leading off the hall. 'If you'd wait a moment, Nurse, I'll tell Madam.'

The room was stuffy and far too full of furniture. Isobel found herself comparing it with the room she had first been interviewed in at Thomas's house and shook her head impatiently. To forget him was going to be impossible, but to encourage thoughts of him was just plain stupid. She stared at a glass case housing three stuffed birds until the door opened and an elderly man came in.

He said rather pompously: 'Nurse Barrington? I'm Dr Snow, Mrs Dalton's physician. I was informed of your coming and wished to see you to give you some idea of her illness.'

He took up a stand before the empty fireplace and cleared his throat. 'She is a sensitive lady, Nurse, and must be treated with great consideration. Her pneumonia is now resolved—antibiotics, of course—but she's always had a great fear of illness and can't believe that she can recover so swiftly. She worries unduly, refuses sleeping tablets as she feels they'll harm her, and as a consequence, sleeps very little. Her domestic staff have done their best but are hardly suitable...' He paused to look at Isobel as though he wasn't sure if she were suitable either. Apparently she was, for he went on: 'She must be kept content, you understand? There's very little nursing care needed; she's able to walk about, take baths and so on, but she requires a good deal of attention.'

He moved away from the fireplace to look out of the window. 'You're prepared to work for seven nights a week? Mrs Dalton dislikes the idea of different faces.'

'Quite prepared, Dr Snow. But I would like to make it clear to my patient that I must leave punctually every morning. If I'm to work each night there can be no question of staying later than half past eight in the morning.'

'Er—oh, yes, I'm sure there can be no objection to that. Now, if you're ready, we'll go to Mrs Dalton.' He added, more pompous than ever, 'I'm a busy man, Nurse Barrington.'

She didn't like him, and she had a horrid feeling that she wasn't going to like her patient either. And she was quite right: Mrs Dalton was sitting up in bed, a large, too fat woman in an unsuitable satin and lace nightgown. There were books and magazines strewn on the elaborate silk coverlet, and a box of chocolates, and a bottle of wine and glasses on a tray on the bedside table. The room was far too warm and smelled strongly of French perfume.

Isobel advanced to the bedside with Dr Snow and was introduced briefly. Mrs Dalton nodded at her, not smiling, her pale eyes screwed up in slow scrutiny. 'You're to come for seven nights a week,' she said.

'Yes, Mrs Dalton, but I've just told Dr Snow that since I'm to be here each night, I must leave punctually in the mornings.'

'I may not be ready for you to go exactly at half past eight.'

'In that case I might suggest that you get a day nurse to relieve me, Mrs Dalton.' Isobel heard Dr Snow's hissing indrawn breath.

'The very idea, when the house is crawling with servants! But I suppose I must agree, although I think it's very inconsiderate of you.' Her pale eyes swivelled to the doctor. 'You'll come tomorrow?'

'Of course, Mrs Dalton; mid-morning, as usual. And now I'll wish you a good night; I'm sure you'll sleep now that you have someone with you. I look forward to hearing better things of you in the morning.'

He didn't bother to say goodnight to Isobel but said loftily: 'I'll see myself out.'

Mrs Dalton, Isobel quickly discovered, was going to be a handful. She had met her kind before, of course, but on a hospital ward where the pithy remarks of the other patients did much to stop the constant complaints and demands. But there weren't any other patients with Mrs Dalton; she was able to keep up a string of complaints and self-pitying remarks and there was no one to stop her. It wasn't nursing, thought Isobel, it was pandering to a selfish woman who wasn't ill any more and who could have quite well done everything for herself. It was almost midnight when Mrs Dalton professed herself ready to try to sleep. 'And you will remain in the room, Nurse, I am sure to wake and need your attention.'

Isobel arranged a chair as far from the bed as possible, set a shaded lamp on a small table nearby and went to the door. 'I'll just go down to the kitchen and see if someone has left a meal for me,' she said calmly. 'I expect you'd rather I had it before you settle for the night.'

Mrs Dalton shot up in bed. 'But I can't be left! I'm ill, I insist…'

Isobel paused at the door. 'I was assured at the agency that I was to work for eleven and a half hours each night with a half hour meal break.' She added gently, 'The hours are very long, Mrs Dalton. I'm not supposed to work more than ten hours a night.'

'Well, I suppose you'd better go down and see,' said Mrs Dalton sulkily. 'I gave no orders, you'll have to find things for yourself.'

There was no need; someone had put a tray ready on the kitchen table, nicely laid out with cold meat and a salad under a glass cover, rolls and butter and a little dish of trifle. There was a thermos jug of coffee too. Isobel sat down thankfully, ate her supper, cleared the tray away tidily and went back upstairs with three minutes to spare. Mrs Dalton was awake.

'Well,' she said, 'I hope you haven't taken too much…'

'A tray had been made ready for me, Mrs Dalton— I don't know by whom. Is there anything else you would like me to do before I turn out your light?'

It was the first of a sequence of difficult nights; Mrs Dalton might be paying big fees, but she expected an awful lot in return. By the end of a week Isobel was almost on her knees, only the thought of the money she simply had to have kept her going. There had been no sign of Thomas; he had probably relegated her to the back of his busy mind, to be remembered in due course when her mother was cured. She was aware that this was an ungenerous attitude, but at least it propped up her pride.

She visited her mother twice during that week, going straight from a hasty breakfast, because she knew that once she had done the chores at home, attended to Blossom's wants and done any shopping, she simply would not have the energy to sustain a bright and cheerful conversation with her mother. As it was, she became almost as pale and thin as she had been while she had been nursing her mother.

It was in the early days of the second week that she acquired another responsibility—a miserably thin and tattered dog which she had found tied to the door of a derelict house on her way home. She had spent a fruitless hour knocking on the neighbouring doors trying to find its owner, but no one wanted to know, and in the end she had gone to the police station where a kindly police sergeant had advised her to give the little beast house room and he would let her know if the owner turned up. 'And that's not likely,' he told her. 'More than likely they did a flit and didn't want to be bothered with the creature. Not much to look at, is he?'

He certainly wasn't; a half-starved mixture of countless breeds with a long wispy tail and a pointed foxy face, his matted black coat sorely in need of attention. Isobel took him home, bathed and fed him, introduced him to Blossom, fed him again and settled him down on an old blanket. He was going to be a nuisance, but he needed a home, and his gratitude was pathetic. Within three days he was a firm friend of Blossom, and showed a flattering devotion towards Isobel.

'Heaven knows what Mother will say when she comes home!' Isobel told him. She had christened him Friday because that was the day on which she had found him, and bought him a collar and lead and a metal tag with his name and address on it. He went to the shops with her and had a quick gambol on the Common in the mornings; not an ideal life, she knew, remembering the long walks she had taken with two dogs which her father had owned years ago, but better than being left to starve on the end of a rope. He was company for Blossom, who after the first rather wary friendliness was now a devoted companion.

At the end of the second week, Dr Snow told her that her services wouldn't be required beyond another week. She felt inclined to point out that her services hadn't really been required in the first place, but discretion held her tongue for her. She had, after all, earned every penny of her money but it had been worth it, she had almost put all of it back into the bank towards Bobby's school fees.

She had taken Friday for his walk, tidied the house and was putting on the kettle for a cup of tea before she went to bed, when the door bell rang. Thomas was on the doorstep, carrying his bag and seemingly unaware of the twitching curtains on either side. He went past her into the tiny hall. 'Tell me, Isobel, do your neighbours watch your every movement? And why in heaven's name, if they want to be curious, don't they have a good look and not just peep round the curtains?' He put his bag down. 'I've taken care to look the part; I wouldn't want them to get ideas about your love life.' He smiled at her. 'My bag makes me instantly respectable.'

She led the way into the sitting room. 'You've come about Mother?'

'No, you. I hear you're working a twelve-hour night seven days a week. That's too much, Isobel. You look…well, never mind how you look, but obviously it's doing you no good at all.'

'How did you know?' she asked.

'Your mother mentioned Dr Snow's name; I happen to have a slight acquaintance with him. You'll give the case up, Isobel.'

There was nothing she wanted to do more, but the arrogance of it put her back up. 'I will not! Besides, I'm to leave at the end of the week.' She added bitterly: 'I don't know why Mrs Dalton needed a nurse in the first place. How is Mother?'

'Making excellent progress—a star patient. Another week and she'll be fit for discharge with an occasional check-up. I recommend a holiday and a return to normal life.'

Isobel stared up at him, all her careful calculations knocked for six. Holidays cost money; she would have to borrow the school fees once again. The doctor, watching her face, knew exactly what she was thinking. He said smoothly: 'We'll worry about that when the time comes, Isobel.' His eye fell upon Friday, who had wrapped himself round Blossom in her basket. 'What on earth have you dredged up there?'

'He was tied to the door of an empty house and no one wanted him. He's company for Blossom...'

'And suppose your next case is one where you have to live in?'

'I'll worry about that when the time comes,' she told him gently.

He said quite violently: 'No, you won't, by God! I'll take him home with me. I've been steeling myself to get another dog ever since old Prince died. Friday seems a fitting substitute and Blossom can come along too for company.' He glanced at the pair of them. 'They'll be splendid company for Nanny while I'm away from home.'

'You're going away?' Isobel hadn't meant to ask, but the words had slipped out.

He gave her a long considered look. 'Only to my

consulting rooms or the hospitals where I have beds. Why should I go away?'

She was tired; too tired to think properly any more. 'Well, on your honeymoon...'

He said smoothly, 'Someone's been talking out of turn.'

'Oh, no—I mean it wasn't servants' gossip, and anyway, none of the people who work for you would do that, and Ella didn't actually say so—but when people get married they have a honeymoon, don't they?'

His eyes were dark flint. If she had been looking at him she would have seen how angry he was. 'It is the normal procedure, yes. Did she tell you where we were going?'

'No, of course not—she didn't actually mention going away with you, only that—that you were kind and considerate to everyone who worked for you and she intended to be the same.'

'And on the strength of that remark, you've come to the conclusion that Ella and I are getting married?'

'Well, you've just been away on holiday with her—and you spent the weekend...oh, that was weeks ago; you did, didn't you?'

He said silkily: 'Oh, yes Isobel, indeed I did. I had no idea you took such an interest in my private life.'

She looked at him without speaking and then because she could think of nothing to say that would help matters—for of what use would it be if she were to say: 'Yes Thomas, I take an interest in you because I love you, even though you're in love with Ella, whom I detest wholeheartedly,' she asked in a polite voice: 'Would you like a cup of coffee or tea? I was just going to make one.'

'No,' said Thomas, and he sounded goaded. 'If you would fetch a lead for Friday and put Blossom in her basket I'll take them with me.' And when she had done that: 'I thought, erroneously it seems, that we'd become friends, Isobel. I know it seemed unlikely at first, but you've grown on me, we seem to have done a lot together. You're a remarkably restful woman, you know.'

She bent over Blossom, not looking up. 'And a good plain cook,' she muttered, and had Blossom's basket snatched from her. 'You have no intention of allowing me to forget that, have you?' he said harshly.

She looked at him dumbly and went past him into the hall to open the front door. What with both of them, Blossom's basket and Friday dancing with excitement, there was hardly room to move.

'I'll see you're kept informed of your mother's progress,' said Thomas, sounding like Dr Winter at his most urbane. 'She should be at the clinic for at least two more weeks, so you can safely take a case outside London.' He looked over her head at the shabby wallpaper. 'Let Dr Martin know if you can't get back here, and we will arrange something. I'll take care of these two.'

'Thank you very much, Dr Winter, I'm very grateful,' said Isobel, addressing the vast expanse of waistcoat inches from her face. 'Goodbye.'

She opened the door. 'Never say goodbye,' he said softly, and kissed her hard.

The little house was very quiet after he had gone. Without the animals she was going to be lonely, but it was much better for them to stay at Thomas's house until her mother was home again and there was someone home all day. She made her tea and went to bed, to lie awake and plan. She would go and see her mother in the morning, tell her that after this week she might not be able to visit her for a while, and somehow, by hook or by crook, she would have to get a case as far away from London as she could. The agency was well known, they often had cases from the provinces, Scotland even. A week or two in some remote place would help her to forget Thomas, or at least come to terms with the situation. She fell asleep at last, quite worn out by sorrow so deep it made sensible thinking an impossibility.

Her mother, when she saw her in the morning, was remarkably cheerful. She was walking alone now, with a stick to give her security, and her speech was almost normal again. She was quite unconcerned about the future and Isobel didn't do more than touch lightly on it. 'I thought I'd get a case outside London, Mother,' she explained, 'now that you're so much better and in such good hands. Mrs Dalton's been a bit trying and I'll look for something easier.'

Her mother looked at her pale unhappy face. 'Yes, darling, do that. I'm quite all right here, and you can phone. It must be lonely at home.'

Isobel was to leave Mrs Dalton on the Saturday.

On Friday morning she went to the agency and found, just for once, the agency lady in an unexpectedly friendly frame of mind.

'Funny you should come in,' she said chattily. 'There's a case at Penn—that's a village just off the M40 near High Wycombe, not all that way away but real country. A six-year-old boy with severe measles. His mother is expecting a baby very shortly and can't nurse him. There's an old nanny there at present, but she can't cope. It wouldn't be a long case, I'm afraid, but the conditions sound pleasant and they're a young family.'

'I don't leave Mrs Dalton until tomorrow morning,' said Isobel.

'That's all right. If you could manage to get down there on Sunday morning—that would give you twenty-four hours.'

It would be a scramble, thought Isobel, but it sounded just what she wanted. 'I'll take the case. How do I get there?'

'If you phone this number they'll come and pick you up.'

'Well, that's a change, and thank you. Would you mind posting on my fees? I'll need some money while I'm there.'

Mrs Dalton chose to behave really badly for her last night. There was nothing wrong with her at all, but somehow or other she contrived to stay awake, demanding drinks, her bed to be re-made, her face sponged, more drinks, until finally she slept. She was still sound asleep at half past eight, and Isobel had no

mind to wake her in order to take an insincere farewell of her. She drank a welcome cup of tea in the
kitchen and left a polite message for her erstwhile
patient with Cook, then she went home.

There was a lot to do—fresh uniform to pack, her
mother to phone, and her new patient's mother, Mrs
Denning, to give her details of exactly how to find
her. This done, she washed her hair, ate several slices
of bread and butter and fell into bed. She was up
again in the evening; there was still her newly washed
things to iron, the house to tidy and another phone
call, this time to Gibson to enquire about Blossom
and Friday.

Both very well and happy, he reported, and uttered
the hope that they would be seeing her soon. She
longed to ask after Thomas too, but there was no way
of doing that. She sent her love to Nanny and hung
up.

She was to be fetched between nine o'clock and
half past in the morning. She got a sketchy supper,
had a bath and went to bed and slept all night, although she hadn't expected to—her head was too full
of Thomas.

A good night's sleep worked wonders. She was up
and dressed and looking almost her usual calm self
when the car arrived—an Aston Martin, driven by a
youngish man with a craggy face, who got out and
looked uncertainly at the miserable little row of
houses. Isobel opened the door and wished him good
morning and, with the least possible fuss, got herself
into the car. The pavement was hardly the place to

introduce themselves; the curtains were twitching like mad, and besides, Mr Denning looked uneasy.

'I'm afraid people like to see what's going on around here,' she explained, and when he laughed, she laughed with him. He was nice, she decided as they drove out of London, going westwards towards the M40. If his wife was nice too, and the little boy, she was indeed in luck.

She heard a lot about Peter, the boy, as they went. 'He's a high-spirited lad,' explained Mr Denning with fatherly pride, 'and he's too much for Nanny—actually she stopped being a nanny some years ago and does the housekeeping, but someone had to look after him. He's very spotty.'

'In bed?'

'I'm afraid so—he's been running a high temperature. He's only been ill for four or five days.'

Mr Denning turned off the motorway and took a country road, and presently reached Penn. It was a charming village, and Isobel sighed happily at the sight of the village green with its pond, and the lovely old cottages round it. The Dennings lived at the far end of the village in a low, rambling red brick house with a large, rather untidy garden, and when he stopped in front of the door it was flung open to allow several dogs to rush out, followed by a pretty woman, who embraced her husband and then turned to Isobel. 'Gosh, am I glad to see you!' she said happily. 'And Nanny will be even gladder. Peter doesn't like being in bed, you see, but he's not very well, she says. Presently, when you've got your breath, perhaps you'd take a look at him. The doctor's coming later this morning.'

Isobel was led inside, through a wide rather untidy hall, and up the stairs to a pretty room overlooking the garden at the back of the house. 'You unpack,' urged Mrs Denning, 'and come down when you've finished—we have to fix things like time off and so on, don't we?! We'll have coffee and then you can go and meet Peter. I'm not allowed near him because of this.' She patted herself gently. 'Only two weeks to go, and we do hope it's a girl!'

Left to herself, Isobel emptied her case, tidied her already neat hair and went downstairs. The sitting room was lovely, full of comfortable chairs, strewn with the Sunday papers and sleeping cats and dogs.

'We're not very tidy,' said Mrs Denning without being apologetic. 'Have some coffee and let's get down to this question of time off. We thought...' She stopped and looked out of the long windows behind Isobel, who would have liked to turn round and look too, only she was too polite.

'There you are!' cried Mrs Denning. 'I suppose you left the car at the front and came round the garden. You're just in time for coffee. And here's Nurse...I can't call you Nurse, what's your name?'

'Isobel,' said Thomas, and came round the back of her chair.

CHAPTER NINE

ISOBEL SHOT ROUND to face him, powerless to prevent the delight surging over her face or the colour flooding it, but her voice was commendably calm if a trifle high as she wished him good morning.

He crossed the room and kissed Mrs Denning's cheek. 'Molly, my dear, as beautiful as ever. How is my godson?'

'Covered in blotches and as cross as two sticks. I don't envy Isobel one little bit.'

'Isobel can cope with most things. Are you going to give me a cup of coffee? Jack's just coming, he's putting the car away.'

'They've only just got here, poor Isobel doesn't know a thing about us or Peter.' Mrs Denning poured coffee and Thomas took a cup over to Isobel before taking his own to an outsize chair between the two of them.

'Isobel and I will go and see Peter together, I can tell her all she needs to know then. Let's see, it's his fourth day, isn't it? I'll go over him just to make sure everything is OK.'

So far Isobel hadn't spoken a word, although she didn't feel out of things. The atmosphere in the room was friendly and when Mr Denning came in and

203

poured himself a cup of coffee and sat down close to her she relaxed nicely under his casual charm, but once she and Thomas were on their own, going upstairs to visit the invalid, it was a different matter. She stopped at the head of the stairs and turned to look at him. 'I didn't know Peter was a patient of yours, Dr Winter—I would have refused the case if I'd known…

He leaned back against the banisters, his hands in his pockets, studying her face. 'I do believe you would, too. Too late now, it's this way.'

He led her down a short passage at the back of the house. 'I saw your mother quite late yesterday evening, she really is doing splendidly. How very fortunate that Bobby has gone straight from school to stay with friends.'

'Yes, it's funny how things turn out—one worries, and there's really no need.'

The doctor grunted, then opened a door and stood aside for her to go into the room, which was large and light and airy, the walls hung with posters and with a bed facing the window. The small boy in it looked suspiciously at her and then whooped with joy.

'Uncle Thomas! I want to get up—say I can! Nanny says no, but she's not a doctor.'

His godfather strolled across the room and leaned over the end of the bed. 'Nanny's quite right, you can't get up until your temperature goes down. Isobel's come to look after you and give Nanny a rest—

she's going to phone me each day, and when she says you have no more fever, then you may get up, not before. Now lie down, there's a good chap, while I take a look.'

Peter allowed Isobel to give a hand, studying her the while. 'You look nice,' he decided finally. 'You're not very pretty, but your mouth turns up and your eyes twinkle. Will you get angry with me?'

'I don't suppose so,' said Isobel. 'I've got a young brother of my own, you see, and I don't suppose you'll do anything outrageous.'

She sat him up and laid him down, took his temperature and finally made him comfortable against his pillows once more.

'It's very dull in bed,' complained Peter.

'Then we'll have to find something to do to pass the time, won't we?' She smiled at him; even covered in red blotches he was endearing.

The doctor put his stethoscope away and wandered over to the window. 'Provided you do exactly what Isobel tells you to do, you'll be out of bed in five or six days, just nice time to see the baby when he or she arrives.'

'I don't really want a brother or sister, Uncle Thomas…'

'Oh, yes, you do—think how nice it will be to have someone to keep an eye on and boss around a bit— an elder brother is very important in a family, you know.' He strolled back from the window. 'I'll be down again in a day or two; look after Isobel, won't you? She's a stranger in these parts. Isobel, come outside while I give you some instructions.'

In the corridor outside he asked: 'Which is your room? This one?' He nodded towards the half open door of the room next to Peter's and when she nodded: 'Good, we'll get things settled, shall we?'

They sat side by side on the bed while he wrote out the routine she was to follow. 'And you must give me a ring if you're in the least worried—young Peter is a favourite of mine.' He turned to look at her. 'You don't look too good yourself—get out as much as you can. Molly knows about time off and so on. You may have to skip your day off this week, though, but they'll make it up to you.' He got up, so she stood up too and, because she felt shy and angry with him too, said the first thing that entered her head. 'How are Blossom and Friday? Did they settle down?'

'Very well—they're being hopelessly spoilt by everyone in the house. They're doing Nanny a lot of good, she's becoming quite active.'

Isobel edged to the door and out into the corridor. 'Please give her my love. I'll—I'll go back to Peter if there's nothing more you want to tell me.'

He smiled faintly. 'My dear Isobel, there's a great deal I want to tell you, but not just now.' He opened Peter's door and she went past him and he closed it behind her without another word.

Peter was a handful, but compared with Mrs Dalton he was sheer heaven. She lost no time in establishing the routine Thomas had laid down, and while she obeyed it to the letter, she found plenty of time to amuse the small boy. Reading was out of the question for him, conjunctivitis was a real danger with severe measles, so she read to him by the hour and when he was bored with that, they made Plasticine models together. She had found two recorders in the nursery adjoining his room, and they played easy tunes together, making a lot of mistakes and rolling around laughing at themselves.

Isobel had been nervous of meeting Nanny, but she soon discovered that the poor dear was only too glad to have a lively boy taken off her hands, although she did sit with him while Isobel took her few hours off each day.

She didn't see much of Mr Denning, who roared away in his car quite early each morning, and roared back home again after tea, but she got to know Mrs Denning quite well—the soul of good nature, anxious that Isobel should be comfortable and happy. They lunched together each day after Isobel had divested herself of the white overall she wore over her uniform while she was with Peter. Strict isolation, Thomas had said, so strict it was.

She hadn't heard any more from him and although Mrs Denning talked about him frequently, she never said anything that gave Isobel an inkling as to what he was doing or where he was.

Probably married by now, thought Isobel miserably. How strange life was, she thought, lying awake in her pretty room. There she had been, bent on get-

ting away from London, putting as many miles between her and Thomas as she could, and what happened? He turned up again. In a romantic novel, of
course, the hero would have arranged the whole thing,
but unfortunately this wasn't a romantic novel, just
unkind fate playing a dirty trick on her. If she hadn't
been so miserably unhappy she would have enjoyed
herself in the Dennings' house. They were kindness
itself. She had time to herself each day, Nanny was
a splendid cook and little Peter liked her. The days
were fine and warm too, and she began to acquire a
pleasant roundness and pink cheeks. It was the kind
of case every nurse hoped to get and so seldom did,
and unfortunately it wouldn't last. Peter was very
much better, the rash was fading and the complications which might have turned a childish illness into
something serious hadn't materialised. She would be
leaving in another week at the latest; there was no
risk of infection now and once he was up and about
his mother would be able to cope with him. He had
a large garden to play in, dogs to keep him company;
another week—maybe less. Isobel went down to
breakfast the next morning quite sure that either Mr
or Mrs Denning would tell her, ever so nicely, that
they wouldn't be needing her for more than another
few days.

She was right, of course, although it wasn't they
who told her. It was Thomas, dropping in on the Saturday afternoon, to lie on the lawn behind the house,
half asleep between his host and hostess. After a

while he had heaved himself to his feet and gone upstairs to see his patient and Isobel.

'You're a fraud,' he told his godson. 'Tomorrow you're going to get up for an hour or so, and in a couple of days you can go into the garden, but only if Isobel says you may, understand?' He turned to Isobel. 'You're out of a job as from next Saturday, Isobel.'

'Yes—well, I expected to be, Peter's made such good progress.' She didn't quite meet his eye. 'And really it will be most convenient. I'll be home to look after Bobby...'

'You won't be taking another case?' Thomas's voice was bland.

'Of course I will, only I'll try to get one where I can live at home.'

'Perhaps I can be of help?'

She said gravely, 'You're very kind, but there's no need. I shan't find it difficult to get another case. Shall I see you before I go?'

He said easily: 'Oh, I daresay!'

'We've said goodbye so many times and then we meet again—it's strange.'

'Very strange,' he agreed blandly. He turned to look out of the window so that she didn't see the gleam in his eyes. 'But of course, I don't say goodbye, Isobel.'

She felt sick at the idea of never seeing him again. She said a little wildly, 'I saw a photo of Ella Stokes in the *Tatler*; she's very beautiful.'

If he was surprised at the sudden change of topic he didn't show it. 'Ella? No, she's not beautiful; stunning, pretty eye-catching if you like. Beauty is something quite different.' He added: 'Do you admire her so much?'

'She's all the things you say.'

'And a great deal more besides. She'll be a very expensive wife—it costs a lot to look like that.'

Isobel said in a strained little voice: 'Well, it won't matter, will it? Someone, I can't remember who it was, told me you had a great deal of money.'

When he spoke his voice was dangerously silky. 'And I suppose this person told you also that Ella and I were to be married?'

'Oh, no—' She hesitated, anxious to say the right thing. 'Well, yes—you see, it was Ella who told me you were rich and she said you were very good to everyone who worked for you and she was going to be like you—very good to everyone too.'

'Did she mention the date of our wedding?' asked Thomas with interest. He looked as though he was enjoying himself.

'No, but why would she tell me, Dr Winter?'

'I can think of several good reasons.' He turned back from the window. 'Have you had a day off this week?'

'No, but I didn't particularly want one. I'm not overworked, you know, and Mr and Mrs Denning are so kind to me. I've been out each afternoon.'

'Good,' he nodded. 'You look better. What's worrying you, Isobel?'

The question was unexpected and she stood staring at him, trying to think of an answer that might satisfy him. She came up with, 'Nothing,' which was of no use at all.

She could see that he wasn't going to leave it there. She was saved from a ruthless questioning by Mr Denning, poking his head round the door to announce that tea was ready and they were having it in the garden—something to which Peter took instant exception, demanding to go into the garden for his tea as well. 'I'll have my tea with you, Peter,' declared Isobel, only too glad to have time to collect herself before another bout of questions from Thomas. But in this she was thwarted.

'That'll upset Nanny,' said Thomas instantly. 'She's been looking forward to having tea with you, I heard her say so. There's jam sponge and she made it specially for you.'

'Oh, well,' said Peter, 'OK, but you won't be long, will you, Isobel?'

'No, love. We'll have a game of Ludo before bedtime.'

Tea was under the mulberry tree at the back of the house—sandwiches, cake and shortbread and scones. 'Nanny's a superb cook,' said Mrs Denning.

'So is Isobel—we fed like fighting cocks when we were in Oslo, and she did all the cooking at Orford.'

Mrs Denning beamed at Isobel. 'My dear, you never said...'

'Isobel is too modest about her perfections,' said Thomas, his mouth full of cake.

He went again before dinner, pleading an engagement in town. He kissed Mrs Denning, thumped Mr Denning on the shoulder and nodded casually to Isobel. To her, 'Goodbye, Dr Winter,' he didn't even bother to reply.

She devoted herself to young Peter for the whole evening, playing one game after another, and then went down to dinner, very bright-eyed and flushed, alternately falling silent and then bursting into conversation. Mrs Denning watched her pretending to eat and, when Isobel wasn't looking, winked at her husband. When Isobel had gone upstairs she said: 'I do hope Thomas knows what he's doing.'

'My love,' said Mr Denning, 'I've known Thomas for a very long time, I've never known him to fall flat on his face, and he won't now.'

'Yes, dear, I'm sure you're right, only I can't help feeling that they're at cross purposes, as it were.'

Her husband considered. 'Isobel is the kind of girl who'll think up all sorts of good reasons why she shouldn't marry a rich man, for a start. She has to be convinced that money is of no importance at all when you're in love. She also has to discover for herself that Thomas isn't and never has been in love with Ella, because he isn't going to tell her—indeed, she may have said something to make him hesitate to do so just for the moment. I think we have to have patience, darling.'

'But she's leaving at the end of the week,' said Mrs Denning fiercely.

Mr Denning picked up his newspaper and hid behind it. 'Yes, dear.'

It was Thursday before Mrs Denning found herself alone with Isobel. Young Peter, up and about and under Isobel's motherly eye, meant that she spent a good deal of time in the garden with him, playing croquet, strolling round tossing a ball, and on the one wet day they had, spending it in the nursery playing endless games of Ludo and sharing the delights of his electric train set. But on Thursday he had been invited to the kitchen to sit with Nanny while she made a batch of cakes, and Mrs Denning, drifting into the living room and seeing her chance, said at once: 'Let's have tea early, we'll go in the garden, shall we? We can have a nice gossip.'

They drank their tea and then ate the fairy cakes Nanny made so well, and talked about clothes and babies and children, and by easy stages through holidays and travel abroad, to Isobel's stay in Sweden and, finally, to Thomas.

'We've known him for ever,' said Mrs Denning. 'Quite brilliant, of course, and works far too hard. Everyone likes him, though he can show a nasty side if he feels like it. I'm so glad he finally finished with Ella—nasty little piece! He's been going off her for months, but she knew how to stick like a limpet, cooking up excuses for him to go to her parents for the weekend, pretending they were ill. I think he was amused at first, and then he got angry. He'd agreed to go to Italy with several friends and somehow or other Ella got herself invited. She did herself a bad turn, actually, because he loathed every minute of it. Of course, we've all known that he'd never marry her, but she was amusing and I suppose he was lonely. He's just been waiting for the right girl to come along.'

'And has she?' asked Isobel in a very small voice.

'Oh yes.'

Isobel, who had hated Ella wholeheartedly ever since she had first met her, formed an instant and strong antipathy towards this unknown creature. She would be blonde, of course—Thomas had admired Ella, hadn't he, and she was blonde...she would be a raving beauty, of course, because she couldn't imagine him falling for anything less than that, and she would have lovely clothes...

Mrs Denning, reading her thoughts accurately, said complacently: 'She's not at all like Ella.' She waited for this to sink in, then, 'We're going to miss you, Isobel—you've been so good, not taking days off and managing Peter so well. I'm sure without you he'd still be in bed with all those complications Thomas kept on about. Are you going to take a little holiday before your next case? Is your mother home yet?'

'No, but I imagine she soon will be, it's wonderful the way she's got better so quickly.' A holiday would be lovely, she thought, somewhere quiet with nothing much to do all day, while her mother got used to living normally again.

She packed her things the next day, played a final game of croquet with Peter, exchanged goodbyes with Nanny because she was leaving quite early in the morning and phoned the agency. No, there was nothing, said the agency lady. She was so sorry, but doubtless if Isobel liked to telephone on Monday there would be something in. Which in a way was nice, as she could have two days at home to see to the garden and her clothes and dust and Hoover. She wondered fleetingly why Mr Denning was so firm about her leaving directly after breakfast. She hadn't liked to ask, because probably they had plans of their own for later in the day. At least he was going to drive her to the station.

It was a beautiful morning when she woke up, and still early. She bathed and dressed, drank her morning tea and packed the last of her things. Mr Denning was a dear, but fanatical about punctuality so she went silently down to the kitchen where a housemaid was beginning on the breakfast and had hers sitting at the kitchen table. That way she'd have more time to say goodbye to Peter. She had already bidden Mrs Denning goodbye the night before and now she went back upstairs to Peter's room. He was awake, doing a jigsaw puzzle in bed.

'I wish you weren't going,' he said the moment she went in. 'I won't have anyone to play with.'

Isobel sat herself on the bed. 'Of course you will! Your mother can play with you now and soon you'll have the baby to keep an eye on, and you'll be going to school in a few weeks. My brother loves school and I'm sure you will too.' She held out a hand. 'So we'll say goodbye for now, shall we? We've had great fun together, haven't we?'

She got up from the bed as Mr Denning came in. 'Ready, Isobel?' His eyes fell on his small son's unhappy face. 'Cheer up, old man, we'll see Isobel again.'

'Really we will?'

'Promise.'

Peter sat up in bed and flung his arms round Isobel's neck. 'Oh, I'm so glad! You're quite the nicest person after Mummy that I know.'

Isobel gave him a rather lopsided smile. 'Well, that's super, Peter.' She kissed the top of his head. 'So I won't say goodbye.'

'That's what Uncle Thomas said to you.'

It was funny how the man cropped up, just when she was trying hard to forget him. She followed Mr Denning downstairs and out of the front door.

Thomas was there, leaning against the Rolls' bonnet, whistling to himself. Isobel stopped at the sight of him and then walked on, for the simple reason that Mr Denning had given her a friendly poke between the shoulder blades.

'Morning,' said Thomas. 'Is this all the luggage?'

'Mr Denning's taking me to the station...' began Isobel in a voice that quavered.

'Well, that was the idea, but I happen to be around and it'll save him getting the car out.' Thomas opened the door and she turned to Mr Denning, all ready to ask questions, only he kissed her quickly and somehow or other she found herself in the car with Thomas, after a brief exchange with his friend, sitting beside her.

'Lovely day,' observed Thomas, and took the car out of the drive and into the lane.

'Delightful,' agreed Isobel, once more her sensible self and lapsed into silence. It wasn't until they reached the M40 and turned on to it that she spoke again. 'We're going the wrong way,' she pointed out.

'No, we're not.' His tone defied her to argue the point, but presently she tried again. 'Are you taking me to another case?' She turned to look at his profile. 'When I phoned the agency there wasn't anything.'

'I know. I asked the woman to say that.'

'You *what*? But I need another job... You can't do things like that!'

'I can, and I do when it suits me. We'll talk about it later.'

'Now,' said Isobel very crossly and then subsided at his even: 'I said later, Isobel.'

'Well, I don't want to talk to you anyway,' she declared with a volte-face which brought a smile to his mouth, and she closed her eyes and pretended to go to sleep. She didn't sleep, of course, her head was seething with a wild medley of ideas which made no sense, and since she couldn't make head or tail of them she opened her eyes again.

They were racing down the M40, going beyond Oxford, a stretch of road she knew well; they would be coming to the exit for Lechlade soon. She gave a little gasp when Thomas slowed the car and turned off the motorway and turned the car again at the familiar signpost pointing down a narrow country road. Hinton Bassett six miles...

Isobel sat upright with a jerk. 'We used to live in Hinton Bassett!'

'I know.' He was maddeningly placid. 'Priory House—the people who bought it from your mother sold it to me a few weeks ago. Your mother is there, and Nanny is keeping her company for a week or so.'

She said in a very small voice: 'Are you going to live there? Mrs Denning said you'd met the right girl.'

'Have I not just said that your mother is living there, and will continue to do so for a great many years yet? I have a fondness for my future mother-in-law, but I don't want to live in her house when I have two perfectly good homes of my own.'

'Your *mother-in-law*?' Isobel's voice was squeaky with a rush of feelings.

'That's what I said.' He added softly, 'My darling girl.'

'Are you—are you asking me to marry you?' asked Isobel.

They were going slowly through the village and

Thomas slowed the car to a stop outside the local stores and post office. He looked around him at the small bustle of a Saturday morning. Several people had paused to look at the car; it wasn't every day that Rolls-Royces actually stopped in their midst. He turned in his seat and looked at Isobel and began to smile. 'Not the best place in the world to propose,' he observed. 'Just think, in years to come when our children want to know how their parents became engaged I shall be forced to say "outside a grocer's shop". No romance, my dear love, and I thought you were romantic!'

'Oh, but I am—if I say yes now, could we drive on and stop somewhere quiet, and you can ask me again?'

Thomas didn't answer her, only smiled with such tenderness that her insides melted, and then he started the car again. He stopped at the top of the gentle hill through the village at a spot where if one craned one's neck one could see the tall brick chimneys of Priory House half way down the valley beyond. He got out of the car and went round and opened Isobel's door. She fell into his arms and he held her close.

'For the second time of asking,' he said, 'but first things first,' and he bent to kiss her happy face.

HOTEL MARCHAND

**Four sisters.
A family legacy.
And someone is out to destroy it.**

**A captivating new limited
continuity, launching June 2006**

The most beautiful hotel in New Orleans,
and someone is out to destroy it. But mystery,
danger and some surprising family revelations
and discoveries won't stop the Marchand sisters
from protecting their birthright…
and finding love along the way.

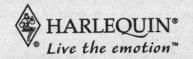

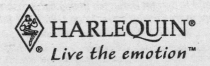